JOE MCFRANCIS

Lifetimes

The Beginning

DFT Publishing

This book was professionally typeset on Reedsy.
Find out more at reedsy.com

Contents

Preface

This series is based on a video game franchise I'm working on, which will be published in the future. Making games is a very slow process.

I decided to make a book series out of the game story because it would give more context and substance to the franchise.

The downside of building a book from a video game script is that it's a work of expanding the screenplay scripts into a different and larger format, which is far from ideal.

This first book has suffered this transformation, more than I expected, because of publishing and format constraints and the consequent tight timeline to perform the expansion work. This caused the screenplay structure to transpire in many parts of the book, and I want to apologise for this. It was a necessary evil to tell you the story in a timely fashion.

Bear with me. The following *Lifetimes* books will be written reversing the process: book first, then the screenplay will be extracted from it. This will make the narrative better structured than this first instalment.

Nonetheless, I'm sure you will enjoy Sophie's adventures. Feel free to subscribe to my newsletter (https://joemcfrancis.com/newsletter/) to be sure to stay in the loop.

Acknowledgement

First and foremost, I want to express my heartfelt gratitude to my family. Their unyielding support and patience throughout the journey of creating this book have been the pillars upon which it stands. Writing is a solitary endeavour, but the cocoon of their love and encouragement has made it less lonely.

A special shoutout to my youngest daughter, Blues. She has graced my life with her presence and lent her sharp eyes and analytical mind to the arduous task of copyediting this manuscript (in a short period of time, mind you. Including this). Thanks to her, every comma is in its right place, and every paragraph sings the tune it was meant to sing. You're a wizard with words, and this book is all the better for your magic touch.

Lastly, thanks to all of you who have embarked on this ride through 'The Beginning' and the Lifetimes series. Readers are the lifeblood of any book, and you've made the endless hours of writing, revising, and worrying more than worth it. Here's to the many more lifetimes of adventures that await us in the pages to come.

With utmost appreciation,
  Joe

I

Part One

Chapter 1

Mother calling me in the morning was the worst part of my day. I love to linger in bed until the last second, which triggers Mom a lot.

"Five minutes, Mom!" I shouted back to her while covering my face with the pillow. Not even 7 in the morning, and school was right down the block, so why? Why? Why do I have to get up this early? Okay, maybe helping prepare breakfast was one of the reasons, perhaps a decent one, but I really, really love to linger in bed!

"Sophie O'Sullivan! Get off that bed!" Mom again! Two shouts later, I dragged myself to the bathroom and started my day. In a flash, I was in school uniform and then downstairs to fry bacon.

Sheila, my bestie, would soon be here to walk to school with me. The senior second year of the Leaving Cert was a real pain, but the idea of finally being done with secondary school and moving to college next year was totally what pushed me on.

My day always started like this, which wasn't too bad. Then, school, homework, and, of course, some hanging with Sheila and the gang. On occasion, I'd even lend a hand in the evening at the pub my family runs. Then finally, ready for bed.

Over the last few weeks, I started to wonder what I should

do with my life. I'm 17 now. I can't spend my life just hanging around and studying. I feel like I'm missing something big, but I can't put my finger on it. All I know is that I'm steadily growing restless, and I don't like it one bit.

* * *

Hanging with the gang every day reminds me that Sheila's the wild one, always looking for trouble for the fun of it. Nothing big, but enough to stir the pot.

On the other hand, Aine was our anchor, our moral compass, always trying to fence Sheila's mess and get us out of trouble.

Niamh was the light one, always brightening up the conversation and steering away from complex or controversial subjects. The girl had a skill for changing topics on the fly without people noticing until it was done.

What about me? Well, if you ask the gang, I am the glue keeping the group together, leading them, mediating choices and the like. If you ask me, I'm the joker of this odd group of friends. I like to run pranks and tell tales once we are done with it. In a way, I'm worse than Sheila in getting us in trouble!

The four of us love to talk about almost anything, and like that goes our time together (when we are not up to pranking people!). We live in an exciting time, so running out of subjects is hard. The world's big guns are always looking to wage war on each other indirectly, using some small country as a battlefield (God forbid actually to face each other for a change!). Eco-terrorists were active these days, picking every reason to blow something up. Just last week, they burned down a pharmaceutical lab where they tested new drugs on animals.

All in all, we couldn't possibly run out of important topics to discuss. Until Niamh shifts the subject to her last boyfriend, the jeans she wants to buy, or when we will watch some old classic movie again.

*** * ***

After school, Sheila, Aine, Niamh, and I were hanging around South Park, one of Galway's loveliest places, if you ask me. This afternoon looks nothing different from any other.

Still, my restlessness grows by the minute. Aine was just telling us how her date went last night, but I was barely paying attention. Instead, my mind jumped randomly from one thought to another, distracting me from the conversation.

"I cannot keep doing this," I said under my breath.

"What was that?" Sheila asked.

"Nothing, sorry. I was just getting distracted. Can't concentrate on the conversation." I said.

"How comes? Is a new lad stealing your thoughts? Who is he? Please, do tell!!" said Niamh, leaning in with a smirk.

"No boy involved. Sorry to disappoint!" I said, "I'm just restless. That's it."

"Nonsense!" Sheila said, "You just don't wanna share!"

"Really! Guys, it's nothing that I can put my finger on. It's just a feeling." I shrugged.

The conversation went on like this for a few minutes; then it shifted to something else, a new subject I didn't really catch.

I was absent, and my imagination was running wild. Flashing colours filled my mind with images of people I had never met. Then constellations and planets spin out of control around stars I don't remember having seen in any book before. All these colours and images were reeling fast, making me feel dizzy. I had to get out of this state, so I got up and decided to part ways.

"Gotta go, guys! I just remembered that I didn't finish the English essay for tomorrow. I really have to get to it and finish it off before dinner. Sorry! See ye all in the morrow!" I said. What a lame excuse that was! But hey, it worked, and I hurried home without giving it a second thought.

I did not take the fastest route home. I walked home slowly and took the longest way. I needed to clear my head, and walking always helped me. Not this time. The odd images kept spinning, colours kept flashing, and I was getting more worried by the minute.

I was no longer in control of my own thoughts! It took me a lot of concentration to keep heading home instead of going in circles. I think I walked around Eyre Square a few times before noticing that I wasn't going anywhere but rather circling the area. In a way, it was both fun and scary.

"Something is very wrong with me, with my head!" I thought at one point, but going crazy isn't something I'd be ready to face. Not by a long shot!

Once home, I went straight to my room, barely acknowledging my parents. I told them the same story about the unfinished essay and added a headache on top of it so that I would just stay in my room and go to bed once I was done with the English piece.

"Do you want me to bring you some tea, dear?" Mom offered.

"Nope, but thank you!" I answered without stopping.

* * *

My room was comforting. It was my personal bubble. The walls were painted in a light blue but covered with posters of my heroes, a total mix of all ages of music and movies: Red Hurley, Larry Cunningham & Country Blueboys, The Beatles, The Platters, Paul McCartney and Wings, and Suzi Quatro, which totally was my favourite, U2, Enya, Pierce Brosnan, and the like.

I closed the blinds to lessen the burden on my eyes and sat cross-legged on my bed. I closed my eyes and dropped my head, focusing on my breathing trying to listen to my heart.

I'm not sure if I stayed there a minute or an hour. The carnival in my head hid from me the passing of time.

At some point, the mesmerising show in my mind slowed down, gradually fading away. Until there was only a starry sky with a big full moon shining its silvery light upon me. And in my head, I saw myself sitting in a vast grassland, still cross-legged, but my back was straight, and my eyes fixated on the moon.

I could actually smell the grass all around me. I could feel the light breeze on my face. The silence was perfect; I could hear my breathing and my heart beating. It was a strangely relaxing situation.

Then, like it was perfectly natural, I was no longer touching the grass; I was floating about a meter from the ground, and it felt natural. The moonlight began to pulse slowly, in sync with my heartbeat. A halo formed around the moon, pulsating along with it. It was like the moonlight was becoming one with my very soul. What an exhilarating feeling!

Was I absorbing the silvery light? It felt that way, but I was also glowing myself! This was the most fantastic daydream I ever had! I was floating, I felt one with everything around me, and I was the moon extension on Earth! I felt like a goddess! "I am Selene, sister of Helios!" I thought, laughing. I really felt like it was real at that moment! It felt great!

* * *

"No, you are not." A female voice said from behind me.

It felt like a scene in a movie when a piece of beautiful soft music is playing, then suddenly interrupted by a vinyl scratching. My floating ceased abruptly, sending my ass to greet the soil beneath the grass. I did not find myself on my bed as I expected. I was still on the ground. Actually, I was gracelessly sprawled on the ground. I looked back. A woman in her 30s was standing there, arms crossed and a smirk on her face. She wore jeans and a polo, her brown hair pulled back in a long ponytail.

"And who the hell are you? And how are you in my head?" I almost screamed at her.

"Good evening to you as well, young lady." She said, that smirk still plastered on her face.

This is getting weirder by the second. Am I trapped in my daydream? How do I snap out of this? I really didn't like it anymore now that Miss Smirky Face 1976 broke the magic.

"Is there something wrong?" Smirky Face asked me.

"Who are you? How comes I'm not awake on my bed?" I asked.

Smirky Face stared at me, clearly amused. But then, she moved, circling to get right in front of me, and she sat in front of me, cross-legged and… floating so as to barely touch the grass.

"You are disappointing me, girl. How can you ask such a question after your ass kissed the ground that hard? How can you still think this is a daydream?" She asked me, with her expression now getting serious, almost grave.

What did she mean by that? If I'm not daydreaming, then where am I? And how? Am I going crazy? Maybe I'm asleep, and this is nothing but a bad dream.

"No, girl. You are not asleep and certainly not dreaming." She said. Was she reading my thoughts?

"Certainly I am, girl." She said, answering my unspoken question.

Okay, now I'm getting tired of this dream. Time to wake up and have a shower.

"No waking up, girl, but I can provide the shower!" She said, the smirk back on her face.

She softly gestured towards me, unfolding her hand with her palm facing the sky, and rain suddenly started to pour - only on me. But when I moved, it followed. So now I'm in a comedy, am I not? Is this supposed to be funny?

"I do see a funny side to this!" Miss Smirky Face said.

"Enough with the name-calling, girl. My names are many, but you can just call me Phoebe, which I like better." She told me as her severe expression returned.

"Okay, so you do have a name. Is that from the old TV series, Charmed? Are you some sort of witch?" I teased her, wearing a smirk of my own just for the fun of it.

"Your ignorance is really something, girl. The name *Phoebe* is ancient, and it was given to me by the ancient Greeks." She said with a scowl. "I'm beginning to suspect that choosing you was not wise of me."

"Okay, lady, this is going too far. Whatever prank you're playing on me, it's time to explain yourself and this whole magic trick of yours." I scowled, feeling somewhere in between angry and scared, two feelings I really didn't care for.

"This is no prank, girl, and there is no magic trick. I am Phoebe, and on this night, I have chosen you as the human vessel to carry the burden of fighting off the upcoming evil. Again, no jokes, no tricks." She said and then snapped her fingers.

* * *

The whole world around us imploded, and in a flash of light, we were now sitting across each other in Eyre Square.

"What about a coffee? Or a Coke? I will definitely have coffee." She said, getting up and heading for the diner across the square. I was still putting myself together, so I didn't even try to answer. I just stood and followed in a state of complete bedazzlement. My face tickled from a drop of cold sweat suddenly rolling towards my cheek.

I wiped it away and took a seat across the table she had selected, still speechless. This was definitely real, but how we got here was totally unreal. I don't like not understanding what happens around me, so I was moving from a state of confused astonishment to one of focused anger. Guess who the focus of that was?

"What about some answers now?" I raised my voice, trying to ignore my fastening pulse.

"What about you tell me what you would like to have? Just a drink or maybe something to eat as well? You know, on a full belly, I suppose we can have a more productive conversation.

My treat!" She said.

"Well, since you're offering, and I'm famished." my pulse quietened, and my body cooled. "I'll have dinner. The lamb stew is delicious here, so I'll take that with lots of coffee." I stared at her and asked, "So, can we talk now?"

"Are you always this hasty? Relax a bit and enjoy this nice evening! We have time, and I think you can learn more from a normal conversation than a third-degree." She said, with a simper now. I suppose I have to play along if I want to get anything out of this lady.

For some mysterious reason, I wasn't as scared as I probably should have been about all the craziness I had experienced until now. This fact alone was unsettling, in a way. I'm not easily frightened, but all this was way beyond normal and natural. Maybe I was in denial, waiting to wake up in my room. Yes, that has to be why I was feeling so normal. Now ordering my preferred meal while sharing the table with some witch, demon, or whatever else this odd character is. What if this wasn't a dream? What if all this is actually happening?

"Sure it is, my dear girl!" Phoebe suddenly spoke with a smile on her face, "And yes, I can hear your thoughts if I so wish. And no, that doesn't prove that this is a dream. It proves that I am who I am."

"Okay, and who would that be?" I asked her, raising a brow.

"Why, I'm Phoebe! Didn't I tell you that already?" She said, laughing at me. She's seriously pissing me off. How can she be like that?

"Do you mind? Either you gimme some serious answers, or I walk out of here right now!" I yelled, slamming my hand on my lap.

"And what makes you think you would be able to walk out

on me? Do tell." Phoebe said, the smirk back on her face.

That was enough, really enough. I got up, and… before I knew it, I was seated again! I tried once more, but again, I kept finding myself sitting.

"Girl, please! People are staring at you now. They will think you had one too many drinks if you keep doing that, don't you agree?" She asked with the most innocent smile on her face. I really didn't like this dream. This is closer to a nightmare at this point, not a dream at all.

"Please, girl, try to relax. Answers will come, I promise. Just don't try to fight it because you just cannot. I'm not an enemy. I do not wish you harm. Actually, I chose you for a high purpose because of your heart, so don't disappoint me." She said to me with a tone that sounded sincere. Then she smiled at the waitress coming up with our orders.

I didn't know what to think anymore, so I concentrated on the food. That was the one thing I knew I could enjoy no matter what. And so I did.

When we got close to finishing our orders, she asked: "Was it that hard to give it a moment?"

"No. But, just to be clear, I'm still pissed at you and this whole thing." I said. I was enjoying the food, but that doesn't mean I'm okay with the rest of what's happening, and I really want her to get that.

"I understand that, but I need you to come to terms with the fact that today, something very special is happening to you. You felt it coming, and it happened. So, while we get to sip our coffee, I'll drop on you way more than the answers to your questions. I will drop the weight of the whole world on you. And that is not a metaphor!" She said with the most severe expression I've ever seen. She was emanating a sense of urgency, a feeling that reached me down to my bones.

That made my anger evaporate, and I felt a strong need to listen to whatever she had to say to me next. How odd was that?

* * *

Dinner was over, and we were now sipping coffee. Phoebe pushed her mug away and said: "Here we go. I'm now going to get you up to speed. Keep an open mind, and do not interrupt me. I will allow questions once I'm done explaining the situation to you and your position within what's going on."

"You must know that humans are not the only intelligent inhabitants of this universe and not the only ones on this particular planet." She said, shifting on her bench.

"There are beings known to humans by many names. Gods and demons are the most common definitions; each has many more, most of them pure fantasy. We have spread some of those myths to ensure our privacy: It is not nice to have half of humanity knocking at your door asking for something every day." She said.

"For those of us who made contact, it has always ended badly, so we had to come up with a way to contain the damage. Humans are not ready to understand other, more evolute sort."

"Some others among us have come to hate the situation and want just to rid the planet of humans. These are considered criminals in our communities, but our laws only allow us to take steps once the damage is done. We tried to change these laws, but it is not a simple process, and we can't get a consensus on how this is to happen."

"We live a very long time compared to humans, and this is why, in human terms, it's taking ages to tackle the issue. But, unfortunately, centuries are meaningless to us, and that, maybe, is part of our problem."

"Now, in this human century, a few extremists are planning what you would call an *apocalypse*, an extinction-level event."

Phoebe was still talking, but my mind wandered away, imagining gods walking among us without us even noticing. The tale she was telling was mind-blowing. The gods are not really 'gods'; they are just a different species sharing the planet with us. In a way, it made sense. I always found it quite ridiculous that almighty gods were human-like. But it made sense that our evolution was similar if they were nothing but a different species sharing our planet.

In a way, all made sense to me, but I still was unsure about the reality of all this. It's likely that I was soundly asleep in my bed and dreaming all this.

"Some of us don't like the idea of genocide, so we must step in and stop those criminals. The problem is that a direct confrontation would be as damaging as the apocalypse they want to bring on. And this is why we have to bring humans into the fight, you in this particular instance." She said, with a sad expression, almost of guilt. And she paused, staring at me. I guess it was my clue to ask questions.

"So you say I'd be your foot soldier in your war?" I asked.

"No, girl. This is your war, not ours. These criminals will be taken care of once they do the damage, and it's only a minor policing thing for us, not a war, not even a bar fight. To make you understand, one of ours creating a human extinction event is like a human deciding to kill all the giant pandas they can find. Would you call that war? No, it's nothing but a criminal trying to destroy an endangered species. Some of us want to step in and empower one or two giant pandas to defend their kind." She explained.

That was an example, alright! Giant pandas? She just compared us to animals! And she is the Green Peace activist in this picture? And I'm the panda she wants to train? This is the most fucked up dream I ever had.

"Do you know how fucking patronising and offensive that sounds?" I said, raising a brow while leaning on the table, pointing at her. "So what is this to you? A charity activity you take up in your free time? You apparently have godly powers, so you want to play god using me as your minion?" I said, lowering my hand.

"Well, girl. That surely is a way to put it. Just know that I have no 'powers'. I just understand the make of the universe, which allows me to exercise some control over it. Humans will get there as well, in time. Your kind focuses more on mechanics, so it'll take more time for you to get to it, but you will. There is no such thing as a godly power. It's all quite natural, part of the evolutionary path." She explained. "Imagine what a Neanderthal would think of your kind today. Imagine that you Homo Sapiens Sapiens had to live among Neanderthals, having to disguise yourselves to avoid shocking them. That is, more or less, the situation between us and humanity. I know that the comparison might sound offensive, but I can assure you, it is not intended as such."

All things considered, Phoebe's words made sense, but I was still kinda sure I would wake up in bed, laughing about this bizarre dream I had. I can't wait to tell the gang about it!

"I'm afraid you won't tell about this to anybody." Phoebe said, "Now it's time to bring you back home, so you can rest." And while she said so, white flashed before my eyes, and we were back in my room. I was sitting on my bed, and Phoebe was standing in front of me. How weird.

"I take my leave now. You will now realise that you were not asleep, and I suggest you make yourself some camomile tea and head straight to bed. Have a good night of rest. Tomorrow I will call again, and we will talk." And saying that, she disappeared. Just like that: she was standing there one moment, and the next, she wasn't.

I decided that the camomile was a good idea, so I went downstairs and made one, thinking about everything that just happened to me. It was all so surreal. I went back to my room and finished my camomile in bed. Oddly, when I laid down, I was asleep in seconds.

Chapter 2

The morning after, I felt great. I woke as usual but did not want to linger in bed. I felt energetic and fully awake. None of what happened last night felt real, but I suspected that it was not a dream, so I decided the best thing to do was to wait. The Phoebe character said she'll be back today, so let's see how this plays out. I got into my school uniform and off I went downstairs to help prepare breakfast.

"Sophie! What is going on? I didn't have to call you, not even once! Do I have to worry?" Mom said to me with a sarcastic tone.

"Mornin', Mom! Not a thing to be worried about. Sorry to disappoint! I'm just famished, so here I am, cooking breakfast!" I said, with a broad smile on my face. It was a good start to the day. I had plenty of time to have breakfast and then go to class with Sheila.

Do I want to tell Sheila about yesterday evening and the whole dream that was not a dream thing? Not sure about that. I had no explanation for what happened, so telling the story would make me look out of my mind. Maybe I better wait and see, so that I will tell Sheila and the gang when I have some more plausible explanation for what happened.

"That is a wise decision," Phoebe said.

Phoebe? Here? At home? I turned around, but she wasn't there. Only Mom and I were here in the kitchen. Was the voice in my head? But it sounded so loud and clear like it was right behind me.

"I am here, but I'm not to be seen nor heard, for now." She said. "You will always be able to hear my voice, but you won't see me unless we are alone. And pay attention not answering me aloud, unless you want to look a tad off the rails. Maybe, in the future, I will also make myself visible to you, but first, you need to get used to this situation. If I let you see me as well so early in the process, it'll be really hard for you to not look at me, and that would give away to others that you are 'seeing things' if you catch my drift!"

"So I have to talk to you in my head? Like this?" I said in my head. I blinked a few times and gulped softly.

"Sure, that will do!" She answered.

"Basically, you're listening to my every thought? Don't you see how rude that is? How can I not feel violated by you doing that to me?" I told her.

This is really gross! Now I have no privacy? I have a whatever-she-is tuned in my every thought?

"I could indeed do that, girl." She said. "But, be realistic: how noisy my life would be if I actually listen to every single thought? That would be MY hell, not yours! What happens, in reality, is that I automatically sense your thoughts when they are about me or addressed to me. Any other thought is squelched."

Well, that makes sense, indeed. Having other people's thoughts in one's head would be a nightmare, indeed.

In all this, what I don't get is how easily I'm adjusting to this craziness. What if I'm just losing it? Statistically, is it more probable that I'm talking to this Phoebe character or that I'm losing my mind? I'm afraid the answer is obvious, so here I need to get less comfortable and begin to be worried.

"Why would you like to worry?" Phoebe said. "Why don't you just ask me to provide some incontrovertible proof? Wouldn't that be easier? I was expecting such a demand from you since yesterday, but, apparently, you prefer to struggle with yourself instead. Go figure!"

Phoebe was making a very good point here, and I suddenly felt like a perfect idiot. Why had that thought not even crossed my mind? Asking for proof is totally the sensible thing to do here. But what proof? What can I ask? She said that their species has control over the fibres of the universe. A really big claim! So I could ask her anything!

"You can, but we are not all-powerful as you might imagine," Phoebe said. "There are universal rules we cannot breach. But yes, do ask freely. Let's see if what you come up with is doable."

Okay, so there are rules. That is good, I think. So what can I ask that can actually qualify as irrefutable proof? It has to be something that others can see and confirm. Otherwise, it'd be just in my head. I think I got it, and it's easy enough, and I won't believe any rule would be broken that way.

"So, lady, I have my request, and this cannot possibly break any rule," I said in my head. "This morning at school, you will trip the main circuit breaker three times at the top of the first three hours."

"Well, girl, you got a very simple one. Deal!" She answered.

* * *

I was really looking forward to this morning's events at school.

19

I was about to find out for sure if I was good for the loony bin or not. It was almost 9 o'clock, just a few minutes to find out. Our English prof was presenting a slide deck about contemporary poetry metrics, explaining the use of iambic trimeter. In the middle of an example, the projector turned off. Everything turned off. The prof tried the lights, unsuccessfully.

"Power's out, class. Let's be patient while the caretaker fixes it in case it's our circuit breaker." the prof announced.

It actually happened! Everybody was chatting, Sheila and I as well, but my mind was looping, "It happened!". So, if it happens two more times, I will have my irrefutable proof of sanity and proof of the existence of my supernatural lady. I was tempted to just accept the first event as proof but to be honest, it could be just a very weird coincidence. So, let's wait and see how this goes.

The next class was Maths. More slide decks, so it'll be easy to see when it happens. If it happens. A few more minutes, and we'll see. It was a refresher class on the unit circle and the practical application of basic trigonometric relationships. So boring! I really hate refreshers.

We were very close now, less than a minute.

Once again, the projector was turned off at the precise top of the hour. Same scene as before. Same 10 minutes of unplanned (but welcomed!) break.

That's two out of three. We officially moved from weird coincidence to incredible coincidence. In one hour we could move into the space of impossible coincidence, so it would be proof of the unthinkable to me.

Sheila and I were chatting about the unreliability of the school's electrical system, and I had to make some effort to keep it normal.

We went back to refreshing our unit circle, but my thoughts were spinning. I was running the possibilities, and they were mind-blowing! Even if Phoebe was just down the basement hand-tripping the main breaker, this was proof of telepathy because the whole conversation about the proof happened in my mind, so that alone was incredible. If the rest was true as well, then I was presented with a totally new understanding of the world we live in.

While immersed in my thoughts, I was brought back to reality by my class laughing and chatting. It was the third hour at the top. The circuit breakers went off again, and everybody made jokes about it. Not me. I was now officially sane, and Phoebe was officially NOT a figment of my imagination.

"Oh, well. Did you really expect a different outcome?" Phoebe's voice asked me, now coming from my side.

In a way, I did hope to be proven insane. At least that wouldn't send my complete knowledge system down the drain. Now I know that we really know nothing at all about us, the planet, the universe and whatever else is out there. We have a whole academic body dedicated to discrediting any supernatural event, so I was just given proof of the inadequacy and ignorance of our academic system. I'm not even sure if the Big Bang theory makes any sense now. As far as I know, we might as well live in a Matrix (remember that very old movie?) or even in a train station locker! What do I know? Nothing! Thank you, odd lady, for destroying my tiny world! For taking away all things I believed to be true! Is Earth orbiting around the Sun? Is Earth almost spherical or flat?

"Are you having a breakdown, girl?" Phoebe asked. "Let me give you some comfort. Planets do orbit around their stars. One or two stars is the most common situation. And no, this planet is not flat. You got that right! About the Matrix thing, I'm not sure that I can deny that because, in a way, it is. Your Einstein went very close to that understanding, so let's agree that the movie is a fantastic exaggeration, but we are made of the same basic material. Finally, I can confirm that I'm not talking to you from a train station and you do not inhabit a locker, but that would be fun indeed!"

* * *

With my mouth agape, I couldn't help but stare at her. So now I know a few things for sure. Phoebe exists, and she has a sense of humour and understands classic movie references. I have been proven sane - to some extent - and the world is not what people think it is. When they say, "we are not alone", they don't really know how true that statement is. We are not the only species and are not at the top of the proverbial food chain. Just yesterday, Phoebe put us at the level of Neanderthals compared to her species.

"Wait now, girl! Don't put words in my mouth, and don't flatter yourself!" She almost screamed. "I never made that parallel. I used the Neanderthals as a cultural simplification to allow you to understand the problem. If we are to make a realistic comparison, I should say that your humanity is to us like microbes are to you. That makes the relationship more clear. The only difference is that you are sentient, so we cannot just destroy you. After all, some quadrillion years ago, we were like you."

"Are you making fun of me now, lady?" I asked, "Because I'm not laughing!"

"But *I* am!" She answered.

As I said before, the lady has a sense of humour. I have to give her that.

So, what now? When will Phoebe get down to business and explain what she meant by me being chosen? Chosen to do what? Are we here in the classic situation where the teenage protagonist will have to save humanity? Phoebe did mention extinction events and did use the word 'apocalypse' so that theme is on the table, I suppose.

So much comes to mind when we think about apocalypses or extinction-level events. We watched so many movies about that subject that our brain has become wired to imagine a horrible pandemic or a giant meteor hitting the planet. And what about zombies? Flesh-eating zombies or the brain-eating variety? Those that move real slow or those that can easily outrun you? And what if it's alien invaders from some far-away galaxy?

I can go on and on listing all the situations our writers and screenplay writers have imagined, but this is now real, and I have no idea what it is. I have understood that if their species actively intervenes, there will be cataclysmic clashes that would determine the end of us. But what can we do, we, the Neanderthal?

These thoughts came to me on and off during the day at school—no way to concentrate on what I was supposed to do in class. I guess I'm going to play the *that time of the month* card and leave school. I'll just stroll to clear my mind before heading home and wait for Phoebe to give me more information about the whole story, finally.

* * *

At least it's a lovely sunny day. I took a very long detour to be able to walk at least an hour. My head needed clarity, and a walk would at least give me some of that. My detour brought me walking on the ocean shoreline. I loved the smell of the salty sea and the sound of the waves on the rocky shore.

I really appreciated this walk. My mind was finally calm, enjoying the mix made by the sun, the light breeze, and the sound and smell of the ocean. I tuned out everything and everyone, just walking about and feeling the day. I could have done this indefinitely!

"Hey, girl! Having some *me-time*, I see!" Phoebe said.

"I knew this couldn't last." I thought. "You can't gimme a break, can you? And, for the record, having conversations in my head still feels borderline insane to me. Can we please find a way to stop this?"

"We could meet more often IRL[1], sure!" She said. "I live in LA[2], but I can come up with a decent reason to spend some time on the old green island! I'll make some calls and will meet you for lunch where we had dinner yesterday. Is that okay?"

"Sure! That would be really great, seriously. Also, please do come prepared to give me context and answer a truckload of questions!" I answered.

It has to be nice to be able to travel from place to place, snapping your finger. No travel visas, no costs, no long lines at customs, no long journeys in tiny seats, and no need for a hotel as one could go sleep home every night. So, not even a need for luggage! That is really a big plus if I could do that I would have visited the whole planet by now!

---

[1] IRL: In Real Life

[2] LA: Los Angeles, Southern California, United States.

Financially there are advantages as well. I suppose Phoebe and her species don't need to work. They can help themselves in so many ways. Sure, most would be borderline illegal to humans, but I suppose they don't really care about that.

I was going wild in my assumptions and fantasies about what Phoebe's species could do and what I would do if I had such power. I suppose I am aware only of a tiny fraction of what they can do, which brings me back to the whole extinction-level event she mentioned yesterday. There are so many things I can imagine having those powers, so it's totally possible that one deranged member of their species could wipe out humankind in an instant. So what's stopping them? Maybe there are rules for them that limit the use of their powers on a large scale? Possibly. So they have to operate on a small scale, which might take time. Okay, there are too many options on the table and too little knowledge about them and their society to pinpoint anything.

"Good!" She said. "It took you quite a lot of thinking, but finally, you realise that you cannot fathom what we can do. Nor which rules apply to us."

"Tomorrow over dinner, I will clear most of the open questions for you." She continued. "Not all of the questions, but enough to get you up to speed on the main matters and the important rules of engagement."

I couldn't wait to have that dinner. Finally, I will understand what this is all about, how I am involved, and why. It's almost incredible that I'm taking all this situation this easy. It's a mind-blowing, life-changing circumstance. I should be on the verge of a nervous breakdown, but no, I am not. I'm almost calm, which makes no sense to me. The sole explanation is that Phoebe is somehow soothing me, making me calmer than I actually would be. I guess all I can do is go home, eat a quick lunch and relax until dinner. Maybe I will push it even to do some homework! Well, I do have to find a way to kill time until my appointment with Phoebe, so it'll be either video games or homework. Did I mention homework before? I really had to be under her influence because I'm totally playing video games until dinner, not doing homework!

While figuring all that out, I changed my direction, so I got home just in time to get something to eat. Mom didn't ask any questions about me not being at school, so I guess it's a good day, or Phoebe is extending her soothing coverage to the people around me. Whatever the reason, I won't complain.

After lunch, I went up to my room, started my PC and got down to spend the rest of the afternoon playing games.

Chapter 3

Dinner time came real fast. One moment, I was playing on my computer, and another, it was already time to go. I got up and changed into fresh clothes real quick. I was really excited to get some answers finally. I still couldn't imagine what was the story here. Phoebe species, some sort of super godly people, was hard to swallow, especially because she looked so ordinary. But what I saw her doing was totally supernatural.

I told Mom not to wait for me because I had dinner with friends and would be late, and off I went. I was almost running, so it took me less than 10 minutes to get to the place. Phoebe was waiting for me at the door.

"Hey, girl! Glad you made it on time! I love punctuality." She said.

"Forget it!" I said, "I'm all but a punctual person. Not sure why I got here on time this evening. Maybe I was not paying attention to the time; I assumed to be late and got here earlier than I thought!"

"We'll see about your punctuality." She said. "Let's get in, get seats and order. Once that part is done, we'll talk."

She drove me across tables, straight to the farthest seats in the corner of the first floor. It was a secluded table, definitely a place where we would talk business without being overheard. She motioned the waitress to come over while we headed for our seats. Once we ordered our dinner, she looked at me with a very grave expression and got started.

* * *

"Okay, Sophie. It is time. You have to understand who I am, what my people are, and why I came to you." She said.

"I presume you know that the universe is not dimensionally finite, as I suppose you heard in school about quanta, relativity, and the natural law not always applicable the way you think."

"Humans are just scratching the surface of the making of the universes, so this will be hard to accept, but please, keep an open mind while I go on. Don't ask me anything until I tell you that you can."

"Living beings are part of evolutionary intelligence. This intelligence begins as micro-individuals with zero knowledge and evolves from there. The species on this planet are all mostly humanoids, but there are so many more species across all universes, so don't think to be unique in any way."

"All sentient beings are on a similar path bringing their inner intelligent spark, the one you may call 'soul', to be one with everything while being a singular entity. Don't try to understand that completely because it's not something you can fully grasp yet, so don't bother, just keep the general concept in mind."

"The spark keeps evolving across multiple changes in state, which humans have called in many ways: reincarnation, transmigration, metempsychosis, rebirth, and so on. the point is that the spark does cross over multiple states of physical existence simply because as long as it's very young it needs a vessel. Otherwise, the spark gets very confused and risks to dissipate, going back into the universal structure to be recycled into a brand new spark."

"During this evolution, the cohesion of the spark with the universes grows. The more it grows, the more it acquires knowledge and understanding of the mechanics of the planes of existence, starting from the one you call the physical plane. This is just like going to school. A car is an unknown object to any child, but once you study how it works and you even get your permit, your knowledge enables you to drive that car. It's no longer a mystery to you. If you see black smoke off the exhaust, you know you are burning oil, and so on. You own it. And if you study mechanics deeper, you can actually repair a car, or even build an engine from scratch, having the tools and the parts."

"Everything works like that. First, humans believed that fire was some magical thing brought by the gods to punish them. Then one of us decided to introduce to your species how to make a fire. In one of your many legends, he was called Prometheus. I suppose you are starting to get where I'm going with this."

"Obviously, way back in time, we were just simple sparks like your ancestors who learned how to make fire from our kin. We are a few hundred millennia ahead of humans, but you will get where we are. That's how it works. Even in the case of an extinction-level event, your sparks will simply move on. Still, such an event can easily have a bad influence on your rebirth, so most of you would be set back for a few millennia. And here I suppose comes in the why I am here."

"Because we cannot directly interfere without doing a lot of damage, those willing to exterminate you humans have to resort to trick humans into doing their job for them. As we speak, some humans have been granted powers in exchange for chaos and war."

"The powers granted to those humans are very limited because nobody wants to risk the Earth survival, so this becomes a matter of balancing the situation by identifying at least one human champion to fight back: that would be you, Sophie."

"I have searched for the right human spark to be safely enhanced, and I only found you, while there are plenty of human sparks ready to become bad news in case of enhancement, but we really don't want that, do we?"

"Given the situation, I cannot guarantee that more than one human will be turned bad, so your position is not going to be easy. On the other hand, your enhancement will be a little stronger than planned, so to give you an edge on the fact that you will be outnumbered in this confrontation."

"I already started your enhancement process. You sure have noticed that your senses don't work as usual. You are more sensitive to everything around you and inside your mind. Buy the end of this dinner, your enhancement will be complete, and you will be ready to begin your training."

"In a moment, I will put in your family's memory that you have won a fully funded study-abroad period, so you will be on your merry way to study in Italy this weekend. Naturally, you will not be studying, at least not for now, but you will be in Italy, where we have a nice school of ours specialised in training for combat as well. You will be joining our school but without full class membership because your powers will be way too low to take the regular classes, but you will be following most of the theory classes, while practice will be carried out separately, just you and your instructors."

"Now you can ask anything you feel asking." She concluded.

At that exact moment, our dinner was served, so I couldn't ask anything right away. I had to wait for the waitress to clear our space, and it was so hard to keep it under control! Phoebe just turned my whole world upside down, and not just that: my life as well. Italy? Really? I have nothing against some more sunny days and pizza, but I would have liked to have a say in all this. Of course, I understand that the situation did not allow such pleasantries, but it would have been nice to ask.

This waitress was the slowest person I have ever seen serving tables, but finally, she went her way.

"That's quite the story you told!" I started. "So your kin is Prometheus, and I guess he's still around? How long do you guys live?"

"Time has no real meaning to us, Sophie." She said. "We have a life expectancy of about to 18 millennia, give or take a millennium or two. And yes, this means that my generation watched men grow from the Holocene to these days. That explains why there are globally consistent legends and myths even for periods when those people couldn't have had any contact. Of course, some of us had fun playing gods, but I guess it was mutually beneficial for a time." She said.

"For a time? Why? What changed?" I asked.

"Don't you remember the history of modern religions?" She said with a sad expression. "Humans grew materialists instead of pursuing intellectual and spiritual evolution. They killed some of us, and when we inspired and gifted some humans to become spiritual guides, they killed them. We live millennia, we are not immortal. We can be killed, and we don't retaliate on such small sparks to avoid damaging your evolution. At least the majority of us."

"That sucks," I said. "You are right; we have killed those guys. There are even fantasy movies about what would happen if a god came here in the present time. It always ends very badly."

"Correct. So you will have to resist the temptation of showing yourself or what you can do. If you do, they will chase you down. You will be captured to be studied and then killed or left to die in a cell on some black site. We still have a policy of non-interference, so we wouldn't be able to help you."

"That sucks even more!" I said. "So, let me see if I get this straight. You are empowering me, and then I will be trained. Once I am sent on my mission, you won't be able to help me if I'm made. It reminds me of those movies where in CIA missions they tell the agents that they are on their own because they never went there officially. Usually, I hate repeating myself, but this is gonna be my mantra: this whole thing fucking sucks!"

"Do not worry; I will personally keep a very close eye on how things progress. I have also considered what additional help we can provide you, and I have already submitted a request to allow you access to some of our automated resources. I know that you will not have full access, but I'm confident you will get more than an extra edge to win this conflict." She said. "For now, look at this as a nice vacation in Italy, an occasion to have fun experimenting with your newly acquired enhancements, and a break from school."

* * *

Back at home, I could tell that something had changed. First, Mom asked me if all was in order for my school trip.

Then something else super-extra odd: I wanted to get a coke can from the fridge, so I turned toward it, and it opened, and the can flew in my hand. Then the fridge door closed itself! Mom did see the whole thing, and it was like nothing happened! What the hell?

"Did you see that, Mom?" I asked.

"What?" She said.

"The Coke can!" I said.

"Well? You don't have to ask permission, I saw you getting one. Why?" She said.

"You saw me get it? From the fridge?" I asked.

"Yes, of course. What's the matter, Sophie?" She answered.

"Nothing, I just thought you didn't, that's all!" I said.

That was really odd. How could she not have noticed what happened? A flying can? So not only does my family think I'm off on s school trip, but I am enhanced with some telekinetic power, and nobody notices when I use that? How does that work? I'm getting really curious. Maybe going to that training in Italy is not a bad idea. I have to get a hold of this enhancement, and I need to know what else I can do before I do some involuntary damage.

"That's the attitude, girl! I knew you were a responsible and cautious person. Well done!" Phoebe's voice said from behind. She was not there.

"Didn't we talk about this?" I said, but just in my head. "Can you not do that, talking to me like you are here when you are not? I'm really sure we talked about that. I really am!"

"I'm so sorry!" She said. "But you see, when you do something really well, I believe it is important to tell you that, to compliment you so that you know I appreciate your responsible behaviour."

"I'm not twelve!" I answered. "I don't need positive reinforcement and validation like a child. That's quite offensive, you know? Stop it. We'll talk when I can actually see you."

And there she was, usual smirk, floating mid-air over the kitchen table. And she waved at me! It took all I had not to react or stare. She was really a sort of a goddess with a hell of a sense of humour. I had to give her that. Excellent timing as well. I guess in all her years on Earth. She learned a thing or two about pranking people and having fun.

And she was showing a wider smirk and waving hard like a hyper child. And was floating up and down like crazy. Okay, she was reacting to my thoughts, making it harder for me to ignore her and stay serious. This lady will be a handful. I wonder if that's a common trait among her species or I had such luck to getting the one.

As though answering me again, she raised her palms, shaking her head like she was telling me, 'who knows? And who cares?'. I just walked away, saying good night to my parents, and headed to my room.

And guess who I found floating above my bed?

* * *

"So, here are a few things you need to know." She said, still floating. "You have been given the ability to command things, which is different from telekinesis. Didn't you notice that multiple things happened in a sequence? First, the fridge door opened; second, the can of coke came to you; last, while the can was coming to you, the door closed. You cannot do that with a single thought using telekinesis. You commanded to have the coke, and everything cooperated to make that happen. That is called *environmental control*."

"Moreover, you shielded your actions from others so that nobody noticed. Actually, their brain processed the event as you simply getting the coke from the fridge as usual. That ability is called *mind projection*."

"So you have discovered two of the enhancements you have been granted. As the name suggests, controlling the environment goes beyond moving stuff to get something, so from now on, you have to take quite literally the saying *be careful what you wish for* because now you are actually making it happen, and that is easily very dangerous."

"But that is not all. You can do much more. Your body has been enhanced, so you now have the physical strength of one of us, which is about thirty times the regular human strength. You haven't broken anything because your brain is aware of the change, and it's driving you to use it correctly without you even noticing. The problem is that if you try to make an effort willingly, you might easily overdo it. My advice is to try a few times to lift something heavy to a human, such as your bed. But don't try to put force in it, because otherwise, you'll cause some damage. Instead, try to lift it like it's really light, as if it were a pen. Do not expect resistance. Go ahead, try."

And so I sat on the floor, grabbed one of the bed's metal legs with one hand, and tried to lift it without expecting any resistance at all. And I did it. I was actually holding my bed with my hand, about half a meter off the floor. I stared at it in disbelief. It was like holding a book, so easy, so light. My body had this incredible strength, but the muscle mass was unchanged. How was that possible?

Like she heard my thought, Phoebe continued.

"Muscle mass is not a factor for us. Your strength is adaptive and comes from the ability to influence the environment. It's hard to explain without getting into maths and physics, so for now, just know that you can easily break anything, so you have to be careful."

"As you can easily imagine, this means you can jump great distances without effort. You can jump on and off a skyscraper if you so wish, but, again, pay attention to what you do because, in the beginning, it's easy to do damage."

"But that's not all. We just scratched the surface of your new abilities. So sit tight and listen because, as you noticed yourself, you have to know what you can do so that you don't get into serious trouble."

We went on for a few hours, talking and experimenting. It was the most intense time of my life. Around 3 AM, Phoebe decided that it was enough for the time being, so she wished me beautiful dreams and vanished.

Like I could sleep now! I promised her to try, and so I got ready for bed. And here I was, lying in bed and staring at the ceiling. I do know that I must rest, especially having used energy I didn't even know I had, but I couldn't find a way to fall asleep. I was way too excited about the whole situation. I was tempted to continue experimenting with my powers. I started levitating under the blankets. It was such fun! Much more fun than going to sleep!

"You promised, girl! Sleep now. Take it as another exercise to get a grip on yourself." Phoebe said. I knew she was keeping an eye on me!

"Okay! Okay! I will try, I promise!" I said out loud.

This is not gonna be easy! But Phoebe had a point, and I

know I have to rest. And I kept trying until I finally fell asleep.

Chapter 4

In the morning, I got up before the alarm went off. I was hypercharged, fully aware of all my new abilities. Well, not all really, but all those we analysed in the evening and part of the night. I felt ready for my training and couldn't wait for tomorrow's flight to Italy. Today will never pass! I will be counting down to the moment I will board the plane.

Now that I think about it, Phoebe didn't say anything about the tickets and the time of my flight. Am I teleporting there? Yesterday, she did mention that I also would have to exercise movement and travel, but we moved on so fast that it didn't have time to sink in. Now, it's surfacing, and I suppose that she meant teleportation. That would be so cool!

Finding out that I had been given all these extraordinary abilities, and she still thought I would need extra help was a haunting thought. How powerful were my human adversaries? Were we evenly matched? Phoebe mentioned something about giving me an edge over my opponents, but that remains quite vague.

I went through the motions all morning and afternoon. Breakfast, school, lunch, school again. I was not great company today, and I suppose the gang felt it. They also asked me about my trip to Italy: I guess Phoebe didn't leave any loose ends.

She had it all planned down to the tiniest details.

The excuse of getting ready for tomorrow's trip allowed me to go home right after school. We had a quick goodbye, but none of us was very good at that, so it was quick and simple. That was lucky because it was so hard to lie to all my closest friends… but what could I do? I cannot disclose any information I received, and I don't want to become a carnival attraction because of what I can do now. This sucks, but I can't tell the truth to my friends, not just because I've been told not to, but because they might mistakenly talk about it with other people, especially Niamh, and the consequences of that are unpredictable, but none of what I can think of is pleasant.

Once at home I went up to my room to start packing. I kept wondering about the means of transportation. Curiosity was getting high on this, especially because I needed to behave like a person about to travel to Italy tomorrow morning, and there weren't many flights from Dublin to Italy.

Also, Italy where? That is a big country, well over ten times Ireland's population and an area over three and a half times Ireland's, with different cultures and even many different languages. I didn't know, but I looked up Italy to learn something about the country before going there. I didn't know that there are twelve different languages officially recognised and many more that their state doesn't want to recognise but are recognised by Italian local governments and globally by UNESCO[3]. Apparently, the Italian language was imposed by law to be learned in school, but many locals still prefer to communicate in their native language. That is gonna be

---

[3] UNESCO: United Nations Educational, Scientific and Cultural Organization

difficult to get used to.

Anyway, overall, I felt so confused, but I could feel the excitement burning in my chest, and I didn't like it, not one bit.

* * *

Phoebe showed up before dinner, floating above my bed as usual.

"Well, Sophie, are you any closer to being ready to go?" She said.

"I'm done packing if that is what you are referring to," I said, "but I still have no idea about how I will get there and where *there* is. This has been bugging me the whole day: mind to shed some light on that?"

"Sure!" She said, smiling at me, assuming a motherly tone. "I will snap my fingers, and you will be *there*, that's it. Everybody will remember that you went to Dublin to catch your flight, so you are covered."

"About where *there* is, I was hoping you'd love to be a surprise. Are you sure you want to know it all? Don't you like a bit of mystery?"

"I think that this week, I've got enough mystery for a lifetime's worth!" I said. "I would really like to know as much as possible from now on, so please do tell."

"Okay, as you wish, my dear." She said. "Your destination is in *Campania*, near *Napoli*. We own a large historical building, a *palazzo*, in a small area known as *Ottaviano*. We bought the *palazzo* from the state a few years back. Actually, we got it on a 99-year renewable concession, which is a way to buy the state's historical estate without talking about a sale."

"Part of it is still open to the public and available for local events because that was the agreement when we got it. A large part of the *palazzo* is private and hosts our training centre."

"In the same area, we also own a few farmhouses on large lots of land. Those are part of the same training infrastructure but used for activities we cannot carry out in the vicinity of human eyes."

"Okay," I said. "Now tell me why you have to teleport me. Why don't you teach me how to teleport?"

"Because that particular ability is all but easy to master." She said. "You will learn it during training, but before you can take the risk to teleport in uncontrolled areas, it will pass quite some time. Do not expect to master it like the simple things we played with yesterday."

"Teleportation is very complex, and you have to excel in its theory first, and only after that you will begin to teleport within the training area, where you can see your destination. Once that is well practised, you will move to transport yourself to a different area in the training centre that you know well, but you cannot physically see. Our personnel will guarantee that nobody will be in the target area."

"Once all that is well mastered on various distances, you will learn how to delay the materialisation phase long enough to look where you are about to land so that you can adjust in case of obstacles present at your destination. That is a very difficult part that can easily take many months of practice before you can safely do it." She concluded.

That made sense, a lot of sense, and made me think. I underestimated the complexity of practising those abilities. Now that Phoebe explained those steps to me, I could clearly see why it was a highly complex thing to achieve, but I didn't before.

That meant I was not thinking straight. I was not keeping my focus on the big picture. This is the kind of mistake that can get me injured, if not killed. I need to practice restraint and kick myself in the butt every time I want to rush into using any of my new powers.

Easier said than done. I'm still a teenager and a minor. I'm having all these grown-up thoughts now, but I guess I'm going to screw things up. How can I keep myself on the ball from now on? This sounds to me much like a New Year resolution. But I have to find a way to actually do it if I don't want to end up making a huge mess. Fuck me!

"Language!" Phoebe said, smiling at me. "I really like the way you are getting the core issues right away. I think I made the right choice by picking you."

* * *

I spent the rest of the evening with my family. I needed a few hours of normality, especially because, starting tomorrow, my new normal was all but a walk in the park. I had tough days ahead of me. In a way, I was scared but also very excited about all the new things happening to me. Most importantly, now I had a significant mission in my life, a meaning that was missing until last week.

So I had a lovely family dinner, we laughed and watched some TV, like nothing was happening. Like I was not going away for a while. It was lovely to discover once again that we, as a family, were still there, loving and appreciating each other. I'm a lucky girl.

When we all headed to our room, we said goodnight, and it was like a new bond was born among us. A soft yet saddened smile stretched my lips, making my heart ache.

II

Part Two

Chapter 5

The following day, I woke up on a very bright morning. Too bright. I opened my eyes and found myself in a bed that was not mine. The room was not mine. The smell was not familiar. It took me a while to realise what had happened. I guess I was teleported to my Italian destination while I was asleep. I suppose false memories were implanted in my family so that all could swear they drove me to the airport and kissed me goodbye.

I'm not good at goodbyes, so I was almost happy that Phoebe did this without discussing it with me. We had a great family night, and that was all I needed. For once, I guess, I was glad that somebody made a decision to make my life easier without bothering to ask. Odd but true.

So, now what? I found my luggage by the bed, so I dressed and went for the door. Exploration time, I guess.

My room was big and featured a high ceiling, but the corridor was huge. It was at least five or six meters wide and very long. I was unsure how long, but no less than 50 meters in each direction. The corridor had a high ceiling with walls covered with beautiful and ornate velvety fabric, but it wasn't wallpaper; it was actual fabric. I walked closely to it, brushing my fingertips along the fabric. It was a mesmerising sensation.

The colours were pastel, soft and balanced, easy on the eyes, and calming to the mind. I wondered if this was real or some sort of enchantment or illusion. I had to ask Phoebe as soon as I saw her. I kept walking until I found a lift. I pushed the call button and waited. When the doors opened, I walked in. A sign advised what was on each floor. I suppose breakfast was served in the canteen on the first-floor mezzanine. I pushed the M1 button, and the lift went down. I reached the mezzanine in a few seconds, and the doors opened, showing me a large canteen. At least thirty or forty students were already there, chatting as happens in any school. I heard many different languages spoken by different groups of students. I noticed that none was wearing a uniform, which was good news: I hate the dress code that includes a uniform.

I got out of the lift and went straight ahead, looking for Phoebe. She couldn't possibly have left me here alone on my first day. I had no idea where to go nor how the canteen worked. Did I need money? Gingerly, I went for the tray's shelf and took one. I was starving, so I decided to go for it, and in case the money was needed, I would tell them to get Phoebe.

There was a large choice of food, continental and not. Also, Asian choice and some others I could not recognise. I grabbed a generous serving of scrambled eggs, bacon, beans, mushrooms, and a large coffee. When I reached the end of the serving line, the lady there, apparently supervising, smiled at me.

"Good morning, Sophie!" she said. "I trust you slept well? My name is Rosalba, the canteen supervisor. Feel free to join your group at table 12H." She pointed in the direction of the table, and off I went to meet my group.

So they knew who I was and had already attached me to a class. Good, it's easier this way. I reached the table. It was the twelfth one on the row, signed with a yellow H sign. Easy system. At the table were already six students about my age. Did they speak English? I really hoped so because that is the only language I know besides the super-basic Irish they have taught us since primary school.

"Hi, Sophie! I'm Bob. Bob Miller," Said to me, a nice dude with dark hair and blue eyes. A work of art if you ask me! And he knew my name! I suppose the class was waiting for the newcomer and was already briefed about me.

"I'm the class rep," he continued, "So anything you need, feel free to come to me. I'm two doors down from your room, so we are neighbours!"

He continued, introducing me to the other classmates at the table. Christine Fleming, a blond with stunning green eyes, and Mark Rogers, who looked like Christine's twin, but nobody mentioned any relationship. Then Stefano Ricciardi, brown hair, tall and wearing an incredible tan, and Nadia Rostov, a redhead who weaved at me with a gorgeous smile. Last introduced was Will Riechter, another stunning guy with pitch-black hair, eyes, and an exceptional smile.

They all seemed like supermodels, ridiculously beautiful. I looked around and noticed that they all were like that! I didn't notice before because the serving area and the food grabbed my attention, but now… I was speechless, and my expression gave that away, I suppose.

"I know," Nadia said. "You are not the first human joining the training centre, and the reaction is always the same. You will get used to our appearance. We are not humans. The youngest among us is Christine. She's 185, while the rest of us are all 186, which is the usual age to join the first year here at the training centre."

My jaw dropped, and my eyes were so wide I thought they popped out. Are these guys all over 180 years old? For real? I honestly had a hard time swallowing that information. I should have expected that because Phoebe told me that this is one of their structures, and I knew that time is nearly meaningless to them, but touching this reality first-hand was shocking nonetheless. I was part of a class of non-human students, all of them way too experienced compared to me. I was still a minor; this was my first time leaving home alone. And these guys have been around for almost two centuries! The things they have seen… the experience they have lived… I will always be looked at as the baby of the group, a baby, quite literally by comparison. I didn't like that, not a tiny bit.

"Okay, thank you for the introductions, Bob, and for clarifying the situation, Nadia," I said. "I'm not sure how I feel about this. No offence, guys, but you could all be my great-great-great-grandparents. It's unsettling, to say the least. I'm sure you can imagine that."

"Sure we do, don't worry!" Stefano said. "You won't feel out of place, I promise!" And he smiled at me with a knowing look. "We are indeed older, but by the measures of our species, we are basically newborns or maybe no more than embryos. And the adults don't shy away from pointing that out every so often. We understand very well how unsettled you feel now, more than you might imagine."

"True!" Mark exclaimed. "Our adults' condescendence is one of the most unnerving things around here! I mean… sure, they are super old, but we have been around a few human lifetimes and experienced them all. Why can a human be considered an adult after just a couple of decades, and we have to wait to be over 2 thousand years old?"

"What?" I said. "You're considered a minor for two millennia?"

"Yes, that's correct," Bob interjected, answering my question. "I cannot stress enough how that is difficult to live with. But I suppose it's all about proportions. To you, 18 years represents about 21% of your life expectancy. In our terms, two millennia is 11% of our average life expectancy, so it's like for a human to become an adult when turning nine. I suppose we are luckier than humans… proportionally!" As everyone laughed at that, I couldn't help but follow: it was funny.

Chapter 6

Apparently, class starts at 9, so we had time to chat some more. Also, I found out that we were the whole class, no others. Seven students in a class were already close to a crowd for the training centre policy.

The class was nothing like what I expected. There was a round table with eight very comfortable chairs, like those only VIPs are allowed to have, all leather, rocking, with recliners, armrests, and headrests. At each seat, there was a laptop case. Each position had a name label.

I took the seat marked with my name and started the exploration of the 'workplace'. I opened the case and found a high-end laptop. I took it out and connected it to the main with its power supply. We had three international power sockets per seat and one of those disappeared inside the table when not in use. My laptop had an Irish plug, and apparently, my fellow classmates had different versions, according to their usual residency, I assumed.

When I lifted the laptop screen, I found an envelope on the keyboard with my name printed. It contained my new username, password, school email address, and instructions on how to set up the laptop.

The first thing to do was to plug it into the network using the cable found in the bag. The network socket was on the right of the power sockets. Once that was done, I turned it on and waited for the process to begin. The usual Windows 11 first setup screen popped up, and in a few seconds, it presented me with the new owner's screen on a background that showed the training centre logo. I filled in all the data, and the system went on, crunching data for a couple of minutes before I was offered a custom login screen. I typed my username and password then the system prompted me to change the password immediately. I had to deal with the usual mandatory password complexity rules that make me crazy, but in the end, I successfully changed my password.

I started exploring my new laptop, and it was insane: 128GB of RAM, 2TB SSD for the boot and 4TB SSD as data disk. The latest CPU, GPU, and 8K resolution on a 17" screen make this a toy positioned at no less than 4,000 Euros. I was more than impressed. I could totally see myself playing my fave games on this jewel!

Looking into the pre-installed software, I found another fantastic set of basically everything one might need to write, present, draw, model or sculpt digitally. Even a games engine was there. Looking into the personal folders, I found my games already installed! Now we are talking!

It was overwhelming. My class was like a C-level conference room, my laptop was the best gaming laptop I've ever seen, and everything was already installed. My mates were almost two centuries old but also cool, like we were really the same age from so many points of view. I was about to run my favourite game when a strong voice filled the room.

* * *

"Good morning, and welcome to my course." The big man said while taking a seat almost across my position.

"My name is Joseph Randall, but you'll address me as Joe," he said. "I am the course coordinator and your combat teacher. Please open your email client and look at your timetable. That is the first email you see chronologically. You also have other communications explaining the policy in place, where to get your training material, how to access the eBooks, and so on."

"As you can see on your timetable, we have our class every morning, for two hours. Teleport classes are daily as well, one hour, twice a day. The rest of the time, you have more traditional subjects, all very important and organised to be relevant to your main training goal."

"Remember, this is not a school; it's a combat training centre. You left school behind when you got here. We are not soft, not understanding, nor will we pamper you like your previous teachers. Here, you will learn to stay alive in heavy combat situations, so consider playtime off the table when we are in session."

"When I tell you to do something," he continued, "it's never a request; it's an order. Non-compliance with any order will be punished in ways you will not like, so let's try not to go there. Now, let's talk about ass-kicking 101."

* * *

Those first two hours were another eye-opening experience. Finally, I got a clear idea of why I was here: to kick the ass of those enhanced humans that were out there causing trouble. The mission was not well defined. My intervention type and its level were supposed to be decided on a case-by-case basis. I will be in charge of that decision because I was supposed to do this alone, on my own.

I learned that the non-human trainees were set to become part of the police force of their species. They only dealt with them, never with humans.

One of the main points of their policy was to never mix with humans when enforcing the law, especially when there was the risk of escalation. The disparity is excessive, and the resulting level of damage could be way beyond expectations, so that was not allowed in any circumstance. I learnt that those directly involved in altercations with humans with serious consequences could easily face a life sentence. I didn't ask what that meant because I didn't really want to know any details of their vision of punishment, especially after I learned that my decision could also involve killing the human I was facing. I was horrified by the idea of killing another person. Joe told me it was okay to feel that way but also clarified that there would be situations where it'll be either me or them, and he preferred to have me alive and them dead if it came to that.

The rest of the day was more relaxing, especially the teleportation classes. Just as Phoebe told me, we studied a lot of theory first. I found out that the two hours a day were organised to have half the time studying the necessary theory and the remaining half practising. We were also told that until the end of the semester, we were forbidden to exercise teleportation outside class.

The day was all dedicated to theory and introductions, as well as in the other classes, such as biology, maths, and physics. I have to admit that the angle of the traditional subjects made them less boring. We always aimed at the practical implication of those subjects in our daily lives as law enforcement. And physics was a real kick from that point of view. Who knew that I needed to understand the very fabric of the matter to be able to use my new powers? Physics wasn't boring at all in this context, and I loved every second of it.

* * *

The day was coming to an end. This new world grasped me so much that time flew by. Lessons ended at 5 PM, so I found myself wondering what to do until dinner: here, they seem to dine late, like 8 PM. I packed the laptop and remembered my games, already installed on it! That is how I'm gonna kill some time now!

"So, what do you plan to do?" Bob asked me while packing his laptop.

"I can't wait to try my game on this jewel!" I answered.

"Playing a videogame? That's your plan?" He said, staring at me with owl eyes and a wildly arched brow.

"Why not? I love playing games. Why is that so odd?" I asked, slightly tilting my head.

"On your first day here, you just found out that you have been selected to represent our law enforcement among humans, and all you want to do is play a game?" He said with a judgmental voice, refusing to look away with his stunned expression.

"Bob has a point, you know?" Christine said.

"I agree. You should come with us." Will added.

"With you where? To do what?" I asked. I was unsure that hanging out with bicentenary people was the right thing to do on day one.

"We want to go out and explore the village," Nadia said. "It seems right to have a look at the place we live in. After all, we are gonna be here for a while, so… let's have a look!"

I was curious indeed, but I didn't really think about exploring an Italian village like that. It wasn't a bad idea.

"Okay," I said. "Taking a quick tour of the village can't hurt. Maybe it'll be even more fun! I'll meet you downstairs in 15?"

And so my gaming session is postponed. But I can't isolate myself, right? So let's go explore the Italian village. I don't speak a single word of Italian, let alone the local language, the Neapolitan. I just hope Italians know some English; otherwise, this will be a very short exploration.

I changed into a more comfortable set of jeans and went down to meet the others.

We walked to the centre of the town. The weather was warm, and the sky was clear. It took less than twenty minutes from our building to the square. The place was really small. The people smiled at us, and some waved. I overheard some conversation, and, as I expected, it was impossible to get a single word: I didn't even catch if it was Italian or Neapolitan.

"Any of you understand a word of what they're saying?" I asked my group.

"We really do not, except for Stefano: he knows many languages and is local!" Bob said.

So Stefano was the language nerd, I guess. At least I was not the only one totally lost in communicating with the locals.

"Any chance the locals speak English?" I asked.

"Not really," Stefano said. "In Italy, we study one foreign language in standard schools, but most Italians study French or Spanish. English isn't that popular yet. Young people do manage some elementary communication, but really super-basic."

Great, so we all depended on Stefano here. Not that it

bothered me much, as long as we could order something to eat. I was feeling a hole in my stomach, the starving kind. I suppose my choice to have a quick and light lunch was not a great idea. Next time I'll eat a proper meal. I guess I was so nervous and anxious to be in class that I didn't really care about lunch. It was my first day here, after all. I was allowed to be anxious. But now I had to eat something.

"Guys, unless you want me to start gnawing on a tree or a chair, we better find a place where we can eat some!" I said, my face expressing all the urgency of my plea. All laughed at my request but were just as starving, so we agreed to get food quickly.

Will pointed at a place, a *bar,* he said, and off he went ahead, motioning us to follow.

The bar was a strange place, not what I expected. There was a long counter, similar to our pubs, but food windows were on each side. A large variety of *panini*[4] on each window and many were not made with bread but with *focaccia.* Maybe it was the hunger, but all looked delicious to me.

Stefano told us to sit at one of the large outdoor tables. He would provide for the order. He asked about the drinks we wanted, and off he went. He spent a few minutes talking to one of the waiters, then came back and sat beside me.

We chatted about our first day, exchanging our initial impressions of the teachers and the syllabus. It felt like all was perfectly normal, like we were a regular class of high school students killing time together. It was really nice. I guess I no longer regret not spending this time playing video games.

After a little while, a waitress arrived with a tray full of *panini*

---

4   Panini: Italian plural for *panino,* which in Elglish is just *panini*

and *focacce*[5], while another waiter served our drinks. A sight to die for!

We all picked randomly from the food tray and wolfed down our prizes. It was really as good as I expected. We all had three serving in a religious silence besides the loud chomping. Why didn't I have this before? Uh, yeah, I'm Irish… we don't have these at home. Our version of a panini pales compared to what I was eating. Actually, the bread and the focaccia used to make them were also new to me. I never had anything similar to this. One thing I totally needed to learn here is how to make these delicious treats.

I had five of them in total, and I had to force myself to stop eating because they were not just delicious but also extra-large. I don't know if the rest of Italy is the same, but they know how to serve a well-sized meal here.

We spent more time walking around the place, exploring. It was a small place but really alive. People were out socialising in the streets, some singing and others even dancing. The place felt really welcoming and warm. It reminded me of places I only saw in movies.

Still chatting and exchanging ideas and thoughts about the day and all we experienced and learned, both in school and out, we headed back to our *palazzo* to hit the bed: it was past 10 PM already.

Halfway to the training centre, we all felt eyes on our backs. We couldn't see anybody, and still, we all felt that.

"Maybe we are all tired and influencing each other," Bob suggested.

"That doesn't seem reasonable," Nadia said. "We are having

---

[5] Focacce: Italian plural for the word *focaccia*.

fun; it makes no sense that all of us are all of a sudden freaking out, feeling eyes on us."

"I agree," Mark said. "There has to be something or someone following us, watching."

We kept moving a tad faster now. I was not sure about *what* we were feeling, but there was something alright.

* * *

After a few more minutes of walking, something flew over our heads. It was fast, black and did not make any noise besides the *whoosh* of its passing and the fast wind it caused.

It couldn't be a bird or a bat because there were no wings flapping noise at all. It couldn't be a drone either because no matter how silent they might be, flying this close, it was impossible not to hear the buzzing of the rotors.

The thing kept flying really fast over our heads for some time that felt like an eternity… maybe less than a minute in reality. Then, it changed its flight schema and started circling around us faster. All we could see was an almost uniform black circle keeping us prisoner. The only sound was the air moved by this thing, nothing else. Now I was getting scared. The others also appeared scared, so I suppose their species is not that all-powerful.

The thing now began to get closer, the circle getting smaller by the second. Nadia tried to jump over, but it was like she had hit an invisible wall. No chance to get out of this by jumping over it. So now what?

While we were contemplating our options, there was another change. Now, the object's darkness was quickly fading until it got to the opposite state, becoming a bright, undefined thing, and the circle visual effect turned into a circle of light. And a column of plasma-like beams formed an actual wall all around us.

"This is getting worse!" Bob said, his face pale, his eyes jittery, trying to catch a glimpse of the thing.

And then the plasma beams started flashing on us. I jolted from the object's first attack. It struck fast, shocking every part of my body it hit. All I could do was defensively raise my hands over my head and groan each time it struck. This went on for only about 20 seconds before it dissolved, but it felt like more than an eternity.

"What the hell?" I said.

We stared at each other, nothing coming out of our mouths. We were confused, angry, and scared, and every inch of our bodies ached like hell.

And now some more, apparently. A spherical light materialised in the middle of the street, blocking our passage. It quickly grew from a small ball to a giant sphere, almost two meters in diameter. It shortly began to fade away, leaving behind a silhouette, a person I couldn't clearly see in the dark.

"Hi, rookies!" the figure said playfully. "That did not go very well, but it was fun. At least for me!"

Chapter 7

Our combat teacher! Joe!

"What was that?" Bob asked, anger oozing from his voice.

"Well, class," Joe started, "that was your official introduction to our trainer device, ZR-1K. The base model is not very difficult to overcome, and it will ambush you now and again until you can get rid of it with ease."

"At that point, you will move up and will be ambushed by the ZS-1V, and that will be an interesting change of scenery for you all. The only time when you will not be targeted will be when you are in class. At any other time, you'll be fair game. Questions?"

"Couldn't you give us a warning? That was seriously scary!" Nadia said.

"Nadia, are you sure you know where you enrolled?" Joe said. "You are in a military training school, not a civilian institution. We train you in combat, not ballet! What? Did you break a nail? You want your mommy?"

"No, Joe," Nadia said, "sorry." She looked beaten, pressing her lips together as she averted her gaze.

I didn't know what to say. I got myself into a really odd and dangerous situation, not really by choice, may I add? I was chosen for this, and now I got a taste of what this training will be: a lot of pain. I suppose that balanced out all the perks I've seen until now.

A military training school? Phoebe never mentioned that to me. She talked about this as a training facility, a school, not the military. I'm no conscript, and I'll have to clear all this up sooner rather than later.

The others were clearly steaming, anger and humiliation written all over their faces.

"Okay, rookies," Joe said, "now I let you go. I'll see you all in class tomorrow morning." And while he said that, he disappeared.

"That was a truckload of horseshit!" Mark said.

"I agree!" we all said, almost in perfect sync. And plasma shots flashed in the night, hitting each one of us.

"Behave, rookies!" Joe's voice echoed in our heads, along with a burst of loud laughter. He was definitely enjoying this.

We all turned silent and got back, walking to our destination: a shower and the bed.

* * *

The shower was great and really helped me to wash off the latest events of the evening. A military facility? This was like a five-star hotel to me, so this new intel about what this place actually is conflicted with everything around me. Well, except for the damn "trainer device ZR-1K", which scared the hell out of me. And hurt!

This thing about being a target all the time hovered over me like a black cloud. I felt like it could attack anytime, anywhere. Until yesterday, I was a high-school student like any other in the human community. Now, all I have are mixed feelings about this whole situation.

Sure, I knew that I was assigned here to be trained in combat, but I didn't expect to end up in a military base, even if it looked like a luxury hotel.

"Phoebe!" I called. "Any chance you can pop in here to clarify a few things?"

Here she was, sitting on the edge of my luxury-barrack queen-sized bed.

"How can I be of service?" She said, smiling. "Are you adjusting to the new place? It's a very nice environment, good food and nice teachers."

"Sure…" I said. "But I guess you forgot to give me a heads-up about what type of facility this is! A freaking military training base? Where we can be ambushed 24/7? Are you fucking kidding me?"

"Oh, that!" She said. "Well, I suppose I did forget to convey to you that small, insignificant, tiny detail… my bad!" And her smile stretched into a wide grin.

"I see that you're having fun!" I said. "I don't really appreciate that kind of detail being missing in your description of my stay here. I was scared to death tonight; all our good times were erased in a jiffy. Not nice at all, especially for the first day in a new place."I said, placing my hands on my hips.

"Oh, please! Stop whining!" She said. "You are not really hurt besides your ego. I told you that this was a place to learn how to fight the upcoming evil, so you could have expected some serious training, couldn't you?"

"What training did you think you would receive?" She asked. "I did tell you about your role, so I might have avoided using plain phrasing, sure. But in the end, you knew this was not supposed to be any kind of vacation, did you not?"

"Sure I did!" I said. "But I've been a civilian until yesterday and a human civilian no less with a high-school straight-A-ish student! How could I have imagined the real meaning of any of this? Can you please forget who you are for a minute and try stepping in my shoes? Do you mind? What else did you not tell me *using plain phrasing?*"

"Fair enough," she shrugged. "I might have left out things that are obvious to me but not so much to you. For that, I apologise. Now, the problem is that I cannot even try to give you the full picture because we are talking about an issue as old as our race. So even a super-condensed version would take too long for you to digest: it's just too much."

"Our race has walked the Earth way before yours. We saw you come to be, and from time to time, we showed ourselves to you to help. For instance, I was known as the Titaness Phoebe to your ancient Greeks. Your people even got close enough to us to learn some of our internal affairs. They distorted the information, but that was the only way they could make any sense of it all."

"If you know your mythology from school, you certainly know that there was a war among us, and a new generation won. Naturally, none of that is true. We did have strong disagreements with our nieces and nephews, and some were quite colourful. We sometimes tend to forget how we can affect your world, so your race saw it as a war. What was, in reality, can be compared to human parents kicking out their kids, telling them to get a life, a job, and to stop taking everything for granted."

"We left them playing 'god' among humans and retired into anonymity. Once on their own, they learned the lesson and experienced the problems accompanying the godlike status with a sentient and very short-lived race."

"Wait a second!" I said, interrupting her with a strong sigh. "Are you telling me that all those gods really existed? All of them?"

Only now I've connected the dots. I feel like an idiot for not getting it since she first mentioned her name and the Greeks. Then she mentioned that some of them were killed. I honestly wrote that off as a truckload of bull. Now she's actually telling me that all those stories were true? All of them? All those religions?

"Not all of them, Sophie," she said. "there has been a lot of confusion in those accounts of what happened. Greeks and Romans mixed up the stories and made some up entirely. They also changed names as they came to them. Other civilizations heard the stories and came up with their localised versions."

"Our actual presence was disclosed to the Maya, the Egyptians, and the Indians. Then we subtly tried to help you, using empowered humans like you, Jesus, or Buddha."

"And please, Sophie, don't start a religion yourself! We had had enough of those experiments, and they all failed. You humans managed to turn all of them into a power machine, destroying all the good of our teachings that we were trying to pass on." She said. Soft wrinkles formed over her brow, and she took a breath.

"Oh well, " I said, "now that you mention it, it wouldn't be that bad to have a woman starting a religion for a change. Let me think about that!"

Her face fell at my pretend decision to think about founding a cult! It was priceless! It took her a few moments to realise that I was teasing her. The last thing I want is to be on the very top of all breaking news on Earth. Then, I'd most likely be nominated public enemy #1, just like all my predecessors.

My predecessors. How odd it feels to be here thinking of taking a job that is in the range of Jesus' abilities. It's like my brain has accepted the situation: it doesn't even feel crazy to be at the same level as Jesus and Buddha. I guess this is how our brain reacts to such an overload of information; otherwise, I would have a nervous breakdown. Still, in a way, it feels kinda absurd.

"Don't make jokes about that!" Phoebe said. "It's too serious to be kidding about it. If anybody finds out what you can do, we will have a serious problem, and I wouldn't know where to begin to fix it."

"Oh, I might have left another.. tiny detail out just because it is a given to me," she said. "You have not really been *given powers.* Instead, your genetic code has been given a push, a sort of accelerated. You do realise the consequences, yes? Or do I have to spell those out to you?"

"Genetic acceleration?" I said. "You mean that I've got an evolutionary jump-start?"

"Yes," she said. "That's one way to put it. The process is not complete yet. It'll take one more week or so to finish the transition. This happens while you are asleep to avoid secondary effects."

"Okay, so I'm a work in progress," I said. "And I suppose the first obvious consequence is that I can never get a DNA test. Is this what you mean by consequences? But I can't really think of any others. Maybe —"

"You got that right, Sophie." She said. "The other consequence is that we are talking about an irreversible process: you cannot go back to being a regular human. We fast-forwarded a set of your natural evolutionary process so that by the end of the week, you won't be a double-helix any longer; you will be a triple-helix. We didn't push you very much, so in a week, your evolutionary rate should resume its regular pace."

"I guess that at on some level, I knew that," I said, lowering my head. "Now, hearing it, it's sinking in, but I knew… Is this going to affect me also physically?" I looked back at her, quickly locking eyes.

"Indeed!" She said. "Your immune system will know much more, so none of the current illnesses will be able to touch you. As a natural consequence, your lifespan is no longer following the human standard: you are looking at at least a couple millennia when the process is complete."

"WHAT?" I accidentally screamed. "You should have started with that! Any other *tiny details* you might have left out? Please, do tell, and don't omit anything if you don't mind!" I clenched my fists, causing my knuckles to turn white.

I braced myself for whatever Phoebe was about to add. Not that a super-long life was bad news, but it changed everything. It'll have so many collateral effects that I can't see right now. I hope they will somehow cover this in my training.

"Well… another natural consequence," Phoebe continued, "is that your muscular tone is changing, along with your basal metabolism and its rate. You will be stronger than humans, much stronger."

"Naturally, this has side effects because your strength won't magically change in a week. There will be a large gap between your potential and your developed strength. As a result, you will feel weak until that gap has been filled. It'll take about a month at the planned rate of your training, so it'll be hard for you to keep up in the beginning."

"There are also many other changes that will happen in your

body and mind, but it's pointless to cover them all this evening. You are spent. You need to sleep now, trust me."

"Like I can sleep now! All this new info is spinning in my head!" I said, sighing softly to calm myself. "But… you might be right. I need to try at least to get some sleep."

We exchanged goodnight, and I was alone again, with a lot going on in my head. I suppose some herbal tea will help me to get some sleep. I went to the corner featuring a kettle and various blends of teas and coffees, started the kettle and began exploring the varieties. I picked a blend of apple and chamomile, which was the right choice. The aroma was soothing. I drank it slowly, sitting in the dark, trying to forget about all that happened today, making silence in my mind and trying to concentrate on the taste and smell of that blessed drink. My eyelids felt heavy after a while, so I put my mug on the nightstand and placed my head on the pillow, drifting away as my eyes shut on their own.

* * *

The sunlight woke me up earlier than I had hoped. I went through my routine without thinking much about last night. Even though I had seven hours of sleep, I didn't feel much rested. I suppose it had something to do with what Phoebe told me—feeling weak until getting at full strength? Maybe it was just the stress of the first day in this place, new people, discoveries and whatnot.

I got ready to roll and headed for the cafeteria to have breakfast, but I was alert, expecting the darn thing to come at me. What did Joe say? That ZR-1K thing could hit anytime besides class timeslots. This is not gonna be as fun as it appeared to be yesterday morning.

In the cafeteria, I grabbed a generous continental breakfast tray and went to our table. Mark and Nadia were already there. We exchanged some lazy courtesy phrases about the morning and the weather, each avoiding mentioning last night's event. I guess nobody wanted to discuss the most embarrassing night of our lives. Well… at least it felt that way!

Anyhow, the first period was with Joe, so avoidance won't last much longer. While we ate and chatted, the others joined the table and the vain conversation about the weather.

* * *

In class, we found Joe waiting for us. He didn't even mention last night. As soon as we were seated, he started with a long lesson about the combat mindset and its relationship with the level of concentration on one's self. Clearly, he didn't want to talk about what - to us - was the pink elephant in the room. We tolerated the class, bored to death by the subject that appeared to be something along the lines of *wax on, wax off*, while some other time, I almost expected Joe to say, "Feel the Force!". Really, maybe I was still too upset to appreciate all the theories about mindset and concentration. The abstraction of one's Id, feeling the surroundings, and being one with the universe.

The whole school day went on very low-key. We listened, took some notes, and wrote down our homework. Nothing seemed to help bring back some of the fun we had during yesterday's classes.

The last period ended, and we went out in a line, looking at each other meaningfully. No need to say a word: we all knew that we had to expect surprises once out of the classroom. Now more than ever, because nothing happened before class, we were all expecting something to happen at any second.

But nothing happened. I was almost disappointed. All the fuss about being *fair game* when not in class, all the tension waiting for an attack, and… nothing.

For now, I decided to go back to my room to shower and relax a bit. I really needed to wash off the anxiety.

I finally reached the door, and I felt a sharp pain in the back of my head. *The hell?* I turned to see what hit me, and another wave of pain stabbed me on my forehead, nearly causing me to lose my footing. I stood my ground before feeling a trail of something wet trickling through my hair. I tried reaching for the pain in my head and felt something liquid. I groaned softly before looking at my fingers, covered in my blood. My vision blurred, and the room began to spin before everything went black.

Chapter 8

I woke up on the corridor floor. One of the trainers (I didn't recall his name) was staring at me. He wore the full tactical gear and his M95 resting like a baby in his arms. He had a grin painted on his face. "Gotcha!" He said.

"What the hell was that!?" I said, groaning loudly at my own booming voice.

"Oh well, you didn't sense me, so those were two nice headshots taken with our training .50 BMG paint-loaded ammo." He said. "They are our design. Of course, they'd kill a human anyway, but for you? Just a terrible headache, don't worry." He added matter-of-factly while he helped me to get up.

My head felt like I had a headbutting contest with a truck. "So, not just the training devices, uh? How nice. Thank you for bringing the party to me." I deadpanned.

"You are very welcome, Ms O'Sullivan! I'm sure you appreciate my humble service." He said, not losing a beat.

"Okay, mister... -"

"Minelli, Marco Minelli, at your service." He said, with a broad smile plastered on his face. To be fair, he looked sincere and friendly. It'll be hard to get used to having the crap beaten out of me by friendly people. But, this was the new dimension

I lived in, redefining the word *friendly* and gods know what else.

* * *

I was in my luxurious room, staring at the red paint on my head. Not blood. Paint. The mirror offered a reflection of me that I couldn't fully digest: I had no sign of the headshots besides the paint. It was unsettling. I stayed there, staring at the figure in that mirror, still not fully accepting what I was becoming.

After one long shower and a change of clothes, I was ready to venture down the canteen to see what they offered for dinner. But I wasn't hungry. The headache was washed out with the red paint, but the feeling of disbelief was still weighing on me. And not just that: what if some other surprise was waiting for me?

Minelli's statement echoed in my mind: *"Oh well, you didn't sense me".* I did not, indeed. I only had one class about *sensing* danger: how can they expect me actually do it? Maybe it was just supposed to be a reflex? Is that part of my ongoing enhancement? Shit! I couldn't make anything out of the training on that subject, and I did not sense a thing. But what about last night? I remember feeling observed before hearing or seeing the ZR-1K. Somehow, yesterday I did sense something. Why not tonight?

Let's think this through. Location? Not likely. I was very relaxed; we were having fun, and I was aware of my surroundings but not consciously. I wasn't *trying* to be on the lookout. Tonight? My mood and attention were different. I was expecting trouble, and I was tired and moody. I kept looking for a threat, consciously, keeping my senses on high alert. Is it possible that this works the opposite way than what I would expect by common sense? Could it be that it only works if I'm not really paying much attention?

"You are getting close, my dear!" said the usual uninvited voice.

"Phoebe!" I almost screamed. "Any chance you can mind your own business for a 24-hour timeframe?" I said with a snarky growl.

"Sorry for the intrusion. I heard Minelli got you well, so I was a little worried about your consequent learning process," she said, "but I see you are making good progress. I'm impressed!"

"Oh? You are, are ya?" I said. "I'm so happy I got your approval! I might wanna throw a party for the occasion!"

"Don't be like that, girl. I'm very concerned about your education process, so I'm glad you did learn from tonight's ambush," she said. "You are not entirely correct on the 'common sense' part," she added. "Think about it a little more. You'll see it's not counter-intuitive. Actually, it makes perfect sense."

"Nope, " I said. "The more I think about it, the more I think that it makes no sense not noticing a threat while paying much attention to it."

"Slow down your thinking," Phoebe said. "Let me give you a scenario." And saying that, with a wave of her hand, a scaffolding board materialised in the room. "Can you walk on this board?" she asked.

"Sure, why should that be difficult?" I said.

"Then do it. Show me how you walk on the board. Walk fast and go from one end to the other and back," she said.

So, not really getting her point, I walked onto the board back and forth. "So what?" I asked. I really didn't understand her point.

"Did you have any difficulties in walking that board? Not so much, I guess?" she said. "So now let's change the venue for one more try," she said, and the usual odd feeling of moving through space and time announced we were going somewhere else.

We were on a small platform, at least 50 meters above the ground. The scaffolding board now connected my platform to another similar one.

"So, girl, you know the drill: walk the board to reach the other side and come back," she said.

"What? That's very dangerous!" I said. "If I miss a step, I can fall all the way down!"

"So? How can you miss a step? You just did it in your room effortlessly!" she said. "Don't be silly. Get on it!"

So, slowly, I moved toward the board and started my journey tentatively, one step at a time. It took me a while to go both ways, and I really did not appreciate the experience. And once I got back to the platform, everything shifted again, and we were back in my room, no board on the floor.

"So, my dear girl, what did you just learn?" she asked me. "Please think before answering."

I suppose I did have to think this through. She was right. When I walked the board in the room, there was no tension. I paid no real attention to what I was doing. I just went on it. Then, when the situation changed and I knew about the risk, I paid attention to every step. I felt insecure. It took ages to go through, one step at a time.

"Are you saying my conscious looking for threats muted my senses this evening?" I asked.

"I knew you had it in you, girl!" She said. "That's correct. That is the difference between yesterday night and tonight. Yesterday you were relaxed, chatting, walking. That's why your senses could work, warning you about what was coming. Tonight, on the other hand, you were so alert, so on the lookout, that you didn't leave space for your senses to work. Hence, the headache!"

"At least one of us is happy, I guess!" I said. Sure, she's right, but I am struggling with how things proceed. I did not expect any of this. Every day there is a new surprise, something else knocking off more of my existence, dragging me deeper into the proverbial rabbit hole.

"Come on, girl! Don't be so dramatic. You are better than that!" Phoebe said. "You are getting stronger every day, transforming faster than we expected, so all this will be easier and easier, don't worry."

"Say that again?" I said.

"What now?" she said.

"The transforming faster thing you just mentioned," I said.

"Oh, that!" She said, avoiding making eye contact. I could swear she was embarrassed.

"So?" I pressed on. "Do tell!"

"I suppose I already told you more than I wanted in the first place," she said, her eyes betraying disconcert. "I don't think you are ready to know all the details. For now."

"Are you testing my patience and temper?" I said. She was starting to piss me off again. This woman had a gift for making me angry. She managed to change my mood into an even darker one.

"You really drop that on me and then refuse to explain?" I said. "You came to me. You decided I am your best choice for reasons

I still fail to understand. Still, you keep condescending, never telling me the whole truth. And now you drop half sentences and won't explain?"

"I have nothing to explain to you because I don't know exactly what to explain, okay?" she said and started pacing in the room. "All we know is that your genetic code is rewriting way faster than we thought possible. It has never happened before, so we don't know what it is and how it'll proceed. So, nothing I can explain until somebody explains it to me. Happy?"

"But you are worried? Is that it?" I said.

"Sure I am! I don't like surprises, especially when the result is a big unknown." She said.

I started to get more nervous by the minute. they lost control of what they put in my DNA? What the hell? "Am I gonna die?" I asked.

"What? No! How can you think that?" she said. "You'll be fine. The thing is that we don't know where your encoding is taking you. Maybe it's nothing at all. Maybe your genetic encoding is moving faster than others because you were already on the evolutionary path by yourself. Who knows? We can only wait and see at this point. Is not that we can take it back, you know?"

"The almighty gods make such big miscalculations?" I said.

"Stop with the 'gods' thing already! We are not gods. We are just people. I explained that to you well enough, so stop. It's difficult as it is already. No need to mock." she said. The way she said it was more disconcerting than the rest of the situation. She seemed sincere, like she believed for real to be 'just people'. Well, I guess it might look that way to them, but by comparison with us humans? Nope, they are totally gods.

"Okay! Fine!" I said, "I won't bring that up again. I promise. I swear on the gods. Oh, wait, that would be you!" I deadpanned.

* * *

Once Phoebe left, I was finally alone with my thoughts. The beautiful room was not appealing tonight. My laptop with my preferred games didn't call for me. I was in a dark mood, sitting on the bed, staring at the window. Almost no lights came in from the outside, so I could see the stars from my bed. I could count those wrapped in the window's view. I almost started counting them for real, but it felt too stupid, so I stared at them, trying to cancel all my thoughts.

We had a few classes about concentration and meditation. The lecturers introduced the basic techniques to begin our journey to full body and mind control. All that *wax-on/wax-off* stuff made me laugh initially, but I could use some mind-clearing right now.

I miss my friends, I mean the gang, back in Galway. Will I ever be able to get back to my life? Will I ever hang out with them again? I never fully realised the implications of this situation. Everything happened so fast, and it was exhilarating. But now? Now I'm digesting it all. The realisation of how deep the wedge between my old self and the new me was dawning on me.

My DNA has changed. I'm training in combat with advanced weapons. And I'm learning to control my newfound 'powers.' They keep telling me that we have no supernatural powers. We just operate on the fibre of the universe around us using our mental muscles, which is not so different from walking or eating. So they say. And the strangest thing is that I can see it now: it's true. The person I am today can no longer go back to the home of the person I was a few weeks ago. And that scares the hell out of me.

I should call Sheila and maybe also Aine and Niamh. But every time I open WhatsApp, I panic and shut it down. All I managed to do was send a couple of messages telling lies about where I was and what I was doing. Then I stopped. I cannot keep lying to the people I love. "What am I gonna do?" I said, muttering to myself.

I kept staring at the stars for a long time, lost in my dark thoughts. I didn't even realise how much time had passed since Minelli took the shot at me. I guess I spaced out because my phone was adamant about being 3:40 AM. I surrendered to the phone and got under the blanket, not even bothering to change into my pyjama. That will be a problem for the day to come. Now, I just wanted to be unconscious. Numb.

I fell asleep in moments, taken away by a short night of restless and dreamless sleep.

* * *

The alarm on my phone forced me awake. It felt like I didn't have the time to fall asleep, and it was time to get up already. I felt tired. Mental exhausted. Something I had never felt before. The sole idea of going to class was killing me. I guess I'm gonna call in sick. I'm just not there. My head felt like the new home to the Mists of Avalon. And I was in the middle of those mists, lost.

I covered my head with the blanket and the pillow, and there I went, looking for the sleep I lost last night. And I almost found it until a loud thumping interrupted my search.

Chapter 9

I barely opened my eyes. What the hell was all that noise? Hammering?

Some of the fog in my brain dissipated, letting me recognise that awful noise: somebody was knocking at my door. Loudly so.

"Go away!" I said. Really, I was not in the mood.

"Cannot do that, Miss." A familiar voice answered from behind the door. I couldn't put a face on it yet.

"Miss?" I said.

"Please, Miss, open the door." That voice again. I could swear I knew who that was, but I couldn't put a face to that voice. I guess I'm still half asleep, and with good reason, if you ask me. "Please, Miss! Don't force me to have the door opened by maintenance."

Who the hell was this? "I'm not well. Leave me alone!" I said, raising my voice.

"That is not possible, Miss. Open this door. Now." The voice answered.

This one's not going to back off. I slid off the bed, my mood worsening by the second, and walked to the door with a big huff, ready to pick a fight.

I opened the door brusquely. The class coordinator, Marlene

something, was there, and she stormed in the second the door opening was wide enough. "Miss O'Sullivan," she said, "why are you not in class? What makes you think classes are optional?"

She was a tiny woman, but her posture and tone made her so imposing and intense that I felt minuscule the second she started talking.

"I don't feel well, Madam, so I decided to stay in bed," I said. "Yesterday's attack was very bad. I didn't sleep enough."

"You are not sick, Miss," she said. "You cannot be. Maybe you feel down, moody, and angry but not sick. So you take your ass downstairs and join the others stat!"

My jaw fell hearing that. "What?" I said, "I feel sick, I need sleep!"

"All you need, Miss O'Sullivan, is to be reminded that this is a military training facility, not a summer camp! Go to class this very second! Do not make me repeat myself!" She said. Her eyes conveyed a determination and strength I never saw before in my short life in Galway. I miss so much my friends and family! I got myself in a sea of trouble.

"Move!" Marlene said, "Now!"

"May I at least change into fresh clothes?" I said.

"You may not," she said. "Next time, change before going to bed. Now move your ass! Go!"

Sluggishly, I went for the door, heading to class. I suppose mentioning breakfast was not advisable. My stomach conveyed all its disappointment about the missing breakfast, which added to my bad mood.

I walked through the corridors, feeling like a zombie, still in my crumpled clothes from yesterday. The missed breakfast made my stomach grumble, and I wondered if I could survive this day. I didn't know how much longer I could take this pressure. I felt like I was sinking deeper into an abyss, and no one seemed to care—nobody except for Phoebe, who was more like a guardian angel than anything else. I couldn't help but wonder if she was really on my side or just keeping an eye on me for her own purposes. It was impossible to know for sure.

As I entered the classroom, all eyes were on me. I could feel their stares, some filled with curiosity, others with contempt, and a few with concern. I tried to ignore them and find a seat, but Marlene's voice echoed through the room.

"Miss O'Sullivan, front and centre!" she commanded. I sighed and dragged myself to the front of the classroom, feeling the weight of everyone's gaze on me.

"Miss O'Sullivan has decided that she's above the rules of this institution," Marlene announced, her eyes cold and unforgiving. "She believes she can skip class when she pleases, and she thinks she can disregard our regulations on appearance. I want all of you to understand that this is not acceptable behaviour. This is a military training facility, and everyone is expected to follow the rules, no exceptions."

I could feel my face burning with embarrassment as Marlene continued her tirade. I wanted to shout that I was a victim too, that I had been forced into this situation against my will, and that I had never asked for any of this. But I knew that wouldn't change anything. In their eyes, I was just another recruit who had signed up for this life and was now trying to shirk her responsibilities.

"Miss O'Sullivan, you will spend the remainder of the day in full combat gear," Marlene said, her voice like ice. "You will participate in every exercise, every drill, and every lesson. You will push yourself harder than you've ever pushed before, and you will not complain. Is that clear?"

I swallowed the lump in my throat and nodded, my eyes stinging with unshed tears.

"Yes, ma'am," I whispered, my voice barely audible.

"Good," Marlene said, her eyes never leaving mine. "Now go get your gear and join your classmates. You're already behind."

I hurried out of the room, my heart pounding in my chest. The weight of my predicament was crushing me, and I didn't know how much longer I could bear it. But as I donned my combat gear and rejoined my classmates, I made a silent promise to myself: I would find a way out of this nightmare. I would find a way back to my old life, my friends and family, and the person I used to be. No matter what it took.

*　*　*

The day was brutal, even more so than usual. Marlene seemed to take a perverse pleasure in making me suffer, pushing me to my limits and then some. I was physically and mentally drained, but I couldn't afford to show any weakness. I had to prove to myself and everyone else that I could do this, that I could survive in this strange new world.

As the day wore on, I thought more and more about Phoebe's words. My genetic code was rewriting itself faster than anticipated, and no one knew what that meant. Was I becoming something entirely new, something beyond human? Or was I simply a freak, a failed experiment destined to be cast aside when my usefulness had run its course?

I couldn't shake the feeling that there was more to this story than anyone was letting on. And despite Phoebe's reassurances, I couldn't help but worry about my future. If I was transforming into something unknown, what would that mean for my chances of returning to my old life? Could I ever truly return to being the person I was before this began?

As the day finally ended, I slogged back to my room, my body aching from head to toe. I had never felt so depleted in my life, and all I wanted to do was collapse into bed and sleep for a week. But as I entered my room, I found a surprise waiting for me: a warm plate sitting on the small table by the window.

I stared at the plate for a moment, my stomach rumbling loudly. I hadn't eaten since the night before, and the sight of food was almost too much to bear. Without a second thought, I dug in, devouring the meal as if it were my last.

I noticed a small note tucked under the plate when I was finished. I unfolded it and read the neat handwriting:

"I know today was tough, but I believe in you. Keep fighting, and remember that you're not alone. - P"

A small, tired smile crossed my lips as I read Phoebe's message. It was a small gesture, but it meant the world to me. At that moment, I felt a renewed sense of determination. I couldn't give up when people like Phoebe were in my corner. I had to keep fighting, no matter how hard it got.

I quickly changed into my pyjamas and crawled into bed, exhausted but determined. As sleep finally claimed me, I made another promise to myself: I would get through this. I would find a way back to my old life and uncover the truth about my transformation. And when I did, I would ensure that whoever was responsible paid for what they had done to me.

As I lay in bed, my mind began to wander. I couldn't help but think about the transformation happening within me, which was so much faster than anyone had anticipated. The notion that my genetic code was rewriting itself was unnerving, and

I couldn't help but feel anxious about what that would mean for my future. I had always been a relatively ordinary person, and the idea that I was becoming something… more, was both fascinating and terrifying.

I tried to imagine what life would be like if I fully embraced these changes. Would I become some sort of superhero, using my newfound abilities to save the world from evil forces? Or would I become a demigod, as the others seemed to believe? The possibilities were endless, yet part of me longed for the simplicity of my old life, a life where I could go out with friends, laugh, and enjoy the simple pleasures of being human.

As I mulled over these thoughts, I realized that I was facing a choice: I could either accept this new reality and embrace the changes happening within me, or I could fight it, clinging to the remnants of my old life and pretending that everything was still the same. Both options had their own appeal, yet neither felt entirely right.

The more I thought about it, the more I came to understand that my transformation was not something I could control. It was happening whether I liked it or not, and there was no going back. I had to face the fact that my old life was gone and that I was becoming something different. Something more. But that didn't mean I had to let go of everything that had made me who I was.

As the night wore on, I began to find some measure of peace in this realization. Yes, my life was changing, and there were many unknowns ahead. But I didn't have to completely abandon the person I used to be. I could still hold on to the memories of my friends, family, and the life I once knew. Those memories will always be a part of me, even if my circumstances have changed.

Slowly but surely, I began to accept the fact that I was in the process of becoming a demigod. I couldn't deny the changes that were happening within me, and I couldn't ignore the fact that my life had irrevocably shifted. But I also knew that I couldn't let fear and uncertainty control me. I had to face this new reality head-on, embracing the challenges that lay ahead and doing my best to adapt to my ever-changing circumstances.

I knew that the road ahead would not be an easy one. There would be many obstacles to overcome, and I would likely face difficult decisions and painful moments. But I also knew that I couldn't let these challenges break me. I had to remain strong, not just for myself, but for the people who believed in me and the greater good I was now a part of.

As I finally drifted off to sleep, I made a vow to myself: I would not let my transformation define me. I would strive to maintain the essence of who I was, even as my life took a new and unexpected turn. And though the path ahead was filled with uncertainty, I would face it with courage, determination, and the knowledge that I was not alone in this journey.

I would embrace my newfound abilities and use them to make a positive impact on the world, but I would also hold onto the memories of my old life and cherish the relationships that had shaped me into the person I am today. My transformation might have been inevitable, but how I chose to handle it was entirely up to me.

The following morning, I awoke feeling slightly more at peace with my situation. I knew I had a long road ahead of me, but I also felt a renewed determination to face whatever challenges came my way. The anxiety and uncertainty that had plagued me the night before still lingered, but I was beginning to see a way forward.

I arrived at class that day with a newfound sense of purpose. Instead of feeling overwhelmed and fearful of my ongoing transformation, I chose to view it as an opportunity to grow and learn. The training sessions were still gruelling, and there were moments when I questioned whether I could ever truly adapt to this new life, but I refused to let these doubts consume me.

As the days turned into weeks, I began to notice subtle changes within myself. My abilities were growing stronger, and I was becoming more adept at controlling them. I was also developing a deeper understanding of the nature of my transformation and the responsibilities that came with it. While I still yearned for the simplicity of my old life, I was slowly coming to accept that I could never go back.

My relationships with my fellow trainees also began to evolve. As we spent more time together, we started to form genuine connections and friendships. I realized that I wasn't alone in my struggles; each of us was grappling with our own fears and uncertainties. As we supported one another and worked together to hone our skills, I felt a sense of camaraderie that I hadn't experienced since my days back in Galway.

There were still moments when I felt overwhelmed by the weight of my transformation, but I found solace in the support of my newfound friends and mentors. They helped me see that while my life had changed unimaginably, I still had the power to determine my path and shape my future.

As I continued to train and grow, I often found myself reminiscing about my friends and family back in Galway, and I made a point to stay in touch with them as much as possible. While I couldn't fully share the details of my new life, I tried to maintain a sense of normalcy in our conversations, clinging to the memories and connections that had once defined me.

The more I embraced my new reality, the more I began to see that my transformation didn't have to be an all-consuming force in my life. Yes, I was becoming something different, but that didn't mean I had to abandon everything that had once made me who I was.

As I faced each new challenge and embraced my growing abilities, I found a sense of balance between my old life and my new one. I was no longer just Sophie O'Sullivan, the ordinary girl from Galway; I was also a trained demigod, a warrior with the power to change the world. While the journey ahead would undoubtedly be filled with obstacles and heartache, I knew that I had the strength and determination to face it all, embracing both the person I had once been and the person I was becoming.

Chapter 10

In the last few months, I grew used to the training and to the daily ambushes. My control over my growing powers was still imperfect, but I no longer feared using them and experimenting. Today would mark a new milestone in my new life: I was about to get my first official mission as part of a real team. Nobody gave me any information about what it was about and the team composition.

After lunch, we returned to class as usual, and each of us found an envelope waiting on the desk. It was the first period of the Strategy class. The teacher waiting for us was a new face. We were all puzzled by this unexpected change to our routine. Nobody said a word. We went to our seats and waited for the teacher to talk. She was a blonde woman in her early 30s, maybe mid-30s, but I know that the actual average age of our faculty members was about 4,200 years, so I guessed she was about 3,100 or so. I still couldn't really get their age right, anyway.

"Good afternoon, class. My name is Captain Ramona Hills." She said. "Today's Strategy class is replaced by the mission briefing on your first assignment. You all have an envelope in front of you. Open it. Read the brief description, then put it back."

I was really excited! My first real mission was about to be presented to me! I opened it gingerly and took out the content. It was a file in a folder. On the folder's cover, there was a "Brief Description" section reading:

Brief Description - Reconnaissance Mission: Operation Starlight

Mission Objective:
To conduct surveillance on a newly identified facility suspected of illegal augmentation procedures, harnessing and exploiting the abilities of demigod entities for illicit purposes.

Agents:

1. ***Sophie O'Sullivan***
2. ***Nadia Rostov***

Location:
Abandoned industrial district, North of Newbridge, adjacent to the Kildare Forest.
Details:
- The facility, codenamed "Nexus", is a heavily fortified three-story structure surrounded by open grounds with minimal external cover.

- Initial intel suggests that there is an underground extension to the facility, the entrance of which remains unknown.

- The region has witnessed a spike in unidentified aerial activities during the nighttime, further bolstering suspicions about the nature of the operations inside "Nexus".
Operational Parameters:

- *The mission is reconnaissance in nature. Engage only if the cover is compromised.*

- *Agents are to leverage their unique abilities to ensure they remain undetected. Sophie's power to manipulate the 'fibre of the universe' combined with Nadia's elemental manipulation will be critical.*

- *Surveillance period should span a day and night cycle, gathering intel on peak activity hours.*

- *Infiltration is NOT recommended unless there is an opportunity to gather solid evidence without engagement.*

- *Collaborative documentation of evidence for the council's assessment and further action.*

Equipment:

- *M95 tactical with silencer and tranquillizer rounds for both agents.*

- *Standard comm device with encrypted channels for immediate communication.*

- *Advanced holographic map of the area with real-time satellite feed.*

Backup:

Agent Marco Minelli is currently on standby for extraction and emergency backup if needed.

Duration:

48 hours, starting at 0600 hours tomorrow.

End Note:

Sophie and Nadia's combined skills are expected to optimize the chances of a successful reconnaissance mission. Prioritizing teamwork, observation, patience, and safety is paramount. Engaging the enemy should be considered only as a last resort. Remember, knowledge is the ultimate weapon—best of luck.

I put down the folder. I was with Nadia, just the two of us. And back in Ireland! That was a nice change of view!

"Class, pay attention." Captain Hills said. "You have received your mission. You are all teams of equals; no team leader is assigned. Remember your training on this subject. Your minds must stay in constant contact, elaborating and coordinating as one single mind. This is a low-risk mission, reconnaissance only."

She went on for two hours, giving us detailed information on the rules of engagement, the safety protocols, the recommended tactics, and so on. The class was dismissed with instructions to dedicate the next two hours as individual teams to study the rest of the folder content and discuss the strategy in detail. Nadia and I decided to have our strategy meeting after dinner in my room.

* * *

I lay on my bed, staring at the ceiling, deep in thought. Beside me, Nadia was fidgeting with some piece of tech, the muted glow from the gadget lighting up her face.

She looked up, her brown eyes inquiring. "Do you know the area?"

A flood of memories washed over me — the scent of fresh rain on Irish soil, the cool breeze, and the sounds of daily life that I took for granted. "I do!" I grinned. "My first mission back to Ireland? That's some serendipitous stuff right there. I can't lie, I've missed home. I know we're not playing tourist, but just being on familiar soil will make things easier."

Nadia smirked, her gaze locked on mine. "Comfort in familiarity? That's cute. Especially after the whirlwind you've been through. You barely got used to having superpowers, and now you're jet-setting on secret missions."

I snorted, "Jet-setting? We're teleporting, and it's not like I have a choice. You're right, though. It's been a wild ride. But hey, at least the food's good here."

Nadia tilted her head, a smirk playing on her lips. "You always did have a thing for the academy's shepherd's pie."

I shrugged, feigning innocence. "Can't help it if they make it just right. Anyway, where do you think we should pop up tomorrow morning?"

Scrunching her nose, Nadia thought for a moment. "Somewhere inconspicuous, I suppose?"

I brightened up, "How about the north side of the forest park? There's this small local road, and believe it or not, an old cafe I used to frequent. Mind you, they don't open till around 9 AM. So, no coffee at dawn."

Nadia groaned. "Of course! The one place you pick, and they don't serve early morning coffee? Are you trying to torture me, O'Sullivan?"

I chuckled, "It builds character, Rostov."

She chuckled, tapping on her tablet. "Alright, north side it is. We'll mark it on the maps for tomorrow. Now, how do we approach this? Stealthy ninjas or the casual stroller?"

"I mean, we're basically looking for weird stuff, right?" I mused, playing with the fringes of my blanket. "The dossier mentioned a probable augmentation training facility. So, odd activities, especially nocturnal ones. Imagine bird-watching, but instead of cute finches, we're looking for half-man-half-whatever-the-hell-they've-made."

Nadia chuckled, "Lovely image. So, bird-watching for monsters. Got it."

I nodded enthusiastically. "Exactly! And, you know, I've

been thinking. Do we really need to be loaded up like some action movie heroes? Why not blend in as, I don't know, nature photographers? At least, that way, we'd have an excuse for the binoculars and stalking."

Nadia raised an eyebrow. "Nature photographers? Seriously?"

"Well, yeah!" I defended. "It makes sense, doesn't it? And it's Ireland—loads of tourists with cameras. We'd just be two more in the crowd. Plus, can you imagine trying to be stealthy with an M95 slung over your shoulder? It's not exactly the subtle approach."

She leaned back, considering. "I see your point. It'd be easier to blend in. Less weight to lug around. And to be honest, I'd feel way more relaxed without having that beast of a weapon."

A grin broke out on my face. "So, we're in agreement then?"

Nadia nodded, "Absolutely. But the captain might have other ideas."

I sighed, "Well, if Captain Hills wants us armed, we'll have to convince her otherwise. We got this."

Nadia smirked, "With your charm, O'Sullivan? Of course."

I rolled my eyes, "You just want that early morning coffee."

She winked, "Guilty."

I chuckled, "Alright, mission 'Ditch-the-M95' is a go."

Nadia laughed, "And maybe mission 'Find-an-Early-Bird-Cafe' too?"

I groaned, "You're never going to let that go, are you?"

She shook her head with a mischievous grin, "Never."

* * *

The grand briefing room always felt like something out of a

sci-fi novel. Massive windows, high-tech projections, and a bit too much of a draught if you ask me. I was standing next to Nadia, attempting to look confident, even though the contents of my dinner begged to resurface.

"You know, for a place filled with demigods, they could've at least installed a decent heating system," Nadia whispered to me, her words fogging in the cold.

"Maybe they assume demigods don't get cold?" I whispered back, suppressing a shiver.

Before I could complain further, in walked Captain Ramona Hills. She was a tall, statuesque woman with radiant blonde hair that flowed flawlessly, even without wind. Honestly, I always suspected some minor deity of haircare was in her lineage.

Ramona cleared her throat, a sound that echoed through the room, rendering it silent. "Alright, ladies. Gather 'round. Sophie, Nadia, front and centre."

We shuffled forward, and I almost tripped over my own feet. Smooth, O'Sullivan, real smooth.

Ramona's lips quirked up, trying to suppress a smirk. "First mission jitters?"

"Absolutely not," I declared too quickly. The room's soft laughter didn't help.

"Captain Hills," Nadia chimed in, her voice steady, saving me from further embarrassment. "The mission dossier mentioned M95s. Isn't that a bit… overkill for reconnaissance?"

"You're suggesting you want less firepower, Rostov?" Ramona raised an eyebrow, a smile playing on her lips.

"Well, not exactly less firepower," I jumped in, "Maybe just… different firepower? Like, say, a camera?"

Ramona laughed. "Ah, Sophie. Always the diplomat."

The holographic display shifted, showcasing the M95s in all their glory. "You have a point, O'Sullivan. But these are not your average M95s. They have been enhanced."

"Enhanced to what? Make coffee?" I quipped, regretting it instantly.

Nadia jabbed me softly with her elbow, but Ramona's chuckle surprised me. "Well, not quite. But considering your request, I think we can arrange a switch. Instead of the M95, you'll receive the latest in photography and audio equipment."

"See? Who needs a gun when you have a camera?" I triumphantly declared.

Nadia added with a smirk, "Especially when the operator is as trigger-happy as Sophie here."

"Hey! That was one time!" I protested, but my cheeks betrayed me, turning a shade of tomato red.

Ramona cleared her throat, drawing our attention. "Focus, girls. This is a critical mission. I know you've trained hard and have powers that give you an edge, but real-world action is unpredictable. Trust your instincts, and trust each other."

I looked over at Nadia, nodding. "Got it, Captain. Stealth, gather intel, and no setting anything on fire."

"Especially the last part," Nadia added, giving me a pointed look.

"The Academy incident was an accident!" I defended.

Ramona chuckled again. "Ah yes, the infamous 'let's see how much heat I can generate' experiment. I read the report."

"You did?" I squeaked.

"She might've shown it to a few of us, too," Nadia whispered, trying to hold back her laughter.

"I think it's charming," Ramona commented, "Your enthu-siasm, that is. But, remember, the aim is to remain unseen, unheard, and definitely not setting anything alight."

With a chuckle, she continued, "You have a gift, both of you. Together, you're a force to be reckoned with. But this mission will test more than just your abilities; it will test your bond. Look out for one another."

"We will, Captain," Nadia affirmed. I echoed her sentiment, still mortified from the earlier revelation.

Ramona's gaze softened, "You might be fresh out of the academy, but I believe in you both. And remember, it's about collecting the intel, but it's also about getting back safely. I won't have two of my best going MIA on their first mission."

"Thank you, Captain Hills," Nadia replied, gratitude evident in her voice.

"As for you, O'Sullivan," Ramona said with a glint in her eyes, "No more experiments without proper supervision."

I sighed, "Yes, Captain."

"And no setting anything, or anyone, on fire."

I pouted, "You make it sound like I do it on purpose."

"Just... be careful," Ramona chuckled.

"We will," I promised.

As the briefing came to an end, I felt a mixture of excitement, dread, and sheer terror. But having Nadia by my side and the unexpected humour of Captain Ramona Hills bolstered my confidence. With a stealthy camera in hand and my fiery (no pun intended) powers at the ready, this mission was going to be one for the books.

Well, as long as I kept the fire to a minimum.

Chapter 11

As the tingling sensation of teleportation ebbed, my feet touched the soft, dew-covered grass. Morning fog enveloped the north side of the forest park, making the surroundings look ethereal. The faint chirping of birds acted as a gentle wake-up call.

I took a deep breath, filling my lungs with the familiar scent of the Irish countryside. "Well, we're here," I remarked, adjusting the camera strap around my neck. The gadget felt foreign but a good kind of foreign.

Looking equally out of place with her oversized telephoto lens, Nadia surveyed the surroundings. "It's so… green," she commented.

I laughed. "What did you expect? It's Ireland. We practically invented the colour green."

She rolled her eyes. "Funny. But you could've mentioned the fog. It's like stepping into a Sherlock Holmes novel."

I chuckled, "You should come around Halloween. It's properly spooky, then. Anyway, cafe's that way," I pointed, "But I've got some bad news."

Nadia frowned, "Don't tell me it's closed?"

"No, worse. It won't open for another three hours."

She groaned, "Three hours without coffee? O'Sullivan, this

is torture. Pure, unadulterated torture."

I grinned, "As I said earlier, it builds character, Rostov."

She mockingly glared at me. "Very funny. So, what's the plan now? Creep around looking for monsters or find another cafe?"

"Well, we could do a bit of both. Scour the place and then get some breakfast," I suggested, glancing at the tree line.

Nadia considered, then sighed. "Fine, but you owe me a proper Irish breakfast. With extra sausages."

"Deal."

As we began our trek, I felt the odd sensation of being back. Here I was, a demigod with superpowers, scouting for potentially dangerous entities, but all I could think of was the picnics I had here as a kid.

"Remember, we're looking for anything out of place," Nadia reminded me, pulling me out of my reverie.

"You mean like that?" I pointed to a squirrel that was, oddly enough, attempting a handstand.

Nadia raised an eyebrow. "That's... not normal, right?"

"Not unless they've started a squirrel circus that I'm unaware of," I remarked, snapping a picture.

We continued deeper into the forest, the sounds of nature our only companions. Every so often, something odd would catch our eye—a bird singing a pop song or a rabbit wearing tiny glasses reading a newspaper. Every peculiar sighting was documented with our cameras.

"Either we're in a weird dream, or this forest has some seriously enchanted critters," Nadia remarked after seeing a frog attempting to play leapfrog with another frog.

"Given our lives lately, I'm betting on the latter," I replied.

For a second, I wondered how people don't notice all this

crazy stuff. Then my training kicked in, and I recalled that time when I wanted a Coke and the fridge opened to let the can fly in my hand, with Mom standing right there, not noticing it at all. That was the first time I heard about *mind projection*, shielding the casual observer from what's actually happening.

Hours seemed to pass, and the sun began to rise higher, dispersing the fog. As it lifted, an odd clearing caught our eyes. It looked too... geometric, almost artificial.

Nadia motioned for me to crouch. "That doesn't seem natural. Think this could be it?"

I nodded. "Could be. Let's get closer."

As we tiptoed forward, an unexpected voice boomed, "Stop right there!"

Startled, we both raised our hands. Turning, we found ourselves face-to-face with a large, burly man dressed in what looked like a park ranger uniform.

"Who are you, and what are you doing here?" he demanded, eyeing our cameras suspiciously.

"We're... nature photographers," I said, trying to sound confident. "Documenting the unique fauna of the area."

He raised an eyebrow. "At the crack of dawn?"

Nadia jumped in, "The early bird catches the worm, right?"

The ranger seemed to consider this for a moment, then snorted. "More like the early bird gets lost in the woods. This is a restricted area."

"We didn't see any signs," I said, hoping he'd buy it.

He grumbled something about tourists always being the same and said, "Alright, off with you. And stay on the marked paths."

Nodding, we retreated, but not before I snapped a quick photo of the clearing.

Once we were safely out of earshot, Nadia sighed in relief.

"That was close."

I nodded, my heart still racing. "Too close. But did you notice? His uniform looked too new, too clean for someone who supposedly works in the woods."

Nadia frowned. "You think he's guarding the facility?"

"I think he's definitely not just a park ranger," I replied.

We decided to circle back to our original starting point. The cafe would be open now, and we both needed some caffeine and food to process everything.

True to her word, Nadia ordered the largest Irish breakfast available while I opted for a more modest portion.

"So," she began, pouring copious amounts of ketchup onto her plate, "We've got squirrels doing gymnastics, singing birds, bespectacled rabbits, leapfrog-playing frogs, and a suspiciously clean park ranger. What's the verdict?"

I sipped my coffee, considering. "I think we're in the right place, but we must be more careful. That ranger, or whoever he was, won't be fooled twice."

Nadia nodded in agreement. "We also need a plan. If there's a facility here, we need to find it, document it, and report back."

"But first," I said, lifting my mug, "We caffeinate."

She chuckled, "Priorities, right?"

"Always," I replied with a grin.

The forest still held many secrets, and we were determined to uncover them. But for now, coffee and breakfast reigned supreme.

Post-breakfast, with our bellies full and our energy restored, Nadia and I sprawled out on a nearby bench. The morning sun was a gentle warmth on our faces. Birds were chirping, and the world felt like it was in no hurry. But we had a mission.

Nadia was fiddling with her camera, zooming in and out

on random things. "You know, Sophie," she began, trying to focus on a bumblebee hovering over a flower, "we've got all this tech on us. Why don't we put it to good use? I mean, besides photographing nature's anomalies."

I glanced over, intrigued. "What do you have in mind?"

She pulled out a small device that looked like a remote. "Drones. My father used to use them for his documentaries. We could do an aerial reconnaissance of that clearing without getting close."

I grinned. "Nadia Rostov, you're a genius. Where'd you get that?"

She smirked, "Snuck it in my bag. Thought it might come in handy."

Deploying the drone was easier said than done. After a few false starts, which included the drone getting stuck in a tree and almost dive-bombing a group of unsuspecting hikers, we managed to get it airborne and stable.

We watched the live feed on the remote's screen, the drone giving us a bird's eye view of the park. The clearing came into focus, revealing a hatch in the ground. Bingo!

Before we could investigate further, the screen suddenly glitched. A moment later, our drone went spiralling out of control and crashed somewhere in the distance.

"Great," Nadia groaned. "There goes our eyes in the sky."

"It's okay," I reassured her. "We've got a lead. That hatch wasn't there by accident. We just need a new plan to approach it."

Nadia snorted, "A plan? Like the one where we blundered into the ranger's path?"

"Hey," I protested, "we got out of that, didn't we? And we learned something. Besides, aren't demigods supposed to be...

unpredictable?"

She tilted her head, considering. "Unpredictable, you say? How about a diversion?"

I raised an eyebrow. "Go on…"

"We make some noise on one side of the clearing, draw their attention, and then sneak in from the other side."

I contemplated the idea. It was bold and a bit risky, but it could work. "What kind of noise?"

Nadia smirked, "Remember the squirrel and the singing birds? We could… amplify their skills. Create a nature concert, if you will."

I chuckled at the image. "A cacophony of critters. I like it!"

We set to work. Using our powers, we gently nudged the forest animals into a performance. Birds started belting out pop hits, the gymnastic squirrel was joined by a few more, and the bespectacled rabbit began reciting Shakespeare.

The "concert" was in full swing. And sure enough, I saw the "ranger" and a few others rushing towards the commotion from the corner of my eye.

We seized our chance and dashed towards the hatch, keeping to the shadows. With a shared glance, we began our descent into the unknown.

But just as we were about to disappear underground, a voice called out. "Excuse me, ladies! Are you the managers of this… unique show?"

We froze. Turning around, we were met by an elderly woman with a broad grin, clutching a small notebook. "Do you think they do private events? My grandson's birthday is coming up, and he'd love this."

Suppressing our laughter, Nadia replied, "We'll see what we can arrange."

As we finally entered the hatch, I whispered, "I told you, unpredictable."

* * *

Our descent into the hatch was nothing like what I'd imagined. It appeared to be a rather plain, metallic entryway from the outside. Inside, however, was a different story. It felt like stepping into a futuristic movie scene; everything was illuminated by soft, glowing lights embedded in the walls, and the air had a faint, sterile scent.

"We're definitely not in Kansas anymore," I whispered to Nadia, looking around.

She nodded, her eyes wide. "Or Ireland, for that matter. This is advanced tech, and it seems a little too fancy for an augmentation training facility, don't you think?"

"It's like a sci-fi spaceship," I mused, walking further in, every sense on high alert.

We traversed through a series of narrow corridors, all the while encountering nothing and no one. As far as secret facilities went, this one was oddly… empty.

After a while, we reached a larger chamber. It was filled with various equipment and terminals, all blinking and humming. In the centre stood a cylindrical tank filled with a mysterious blue liquid. Suspended within was a human figure.

I gasped. "Is that…?"

"A human in stasis?" Nadia finished, approaching the tank cautiously. "Looks like it. And if I'm not wrong, that's a type of augmentation process."

I gulped. "Looks like our intel was correct."

We needed evidence, so Nadia began snapping pictures of

everything, ensuring the flash was off so as not to alert anyone.

"Remember when we had to shoot a short film for the academy's annual festival?" Nadia said, adjusting the camera's lens, "Who would've thought it would come in handy during a reconnaissance mission?"

I chuckled. "And remember when you made me wear that ridiculous alien costume?"

Nadia grinned, her eyes gleaming. "Hey, it was a hit! Though right now, we're kind of living our own sci-fi adventure."

"Let's just hope it doesn't turn into a horror," I retorted, checking the corridor we came from.

Suddenly, a loud siren began to wail, and red lights flashed around the chamber.

"They know we're here," I said, grabbing Nadia's arm.

"We need to get out, and fast," she replied.

Using our demigod skills, we tried to outpace whatever security measures were in place. As we sprinted through the maze-like corridors, alarms continued to blare, and a metallic voice echoed through the facility, "Intruders detected. Initiating containment protocols."

Suddenly, a set of doors slammed shut in front of us. We skidded to a stop, almost crashing into them.

"That's not good," Nadia said, slightly out of breath.

Looking around, Nadia spotted a ventilation shaft above. "Up there! We can crawl our way out!" She grimaced. "Not my preferred method of exit, but beggars can't be choosers."

We quickly climbed into the shaft, navigating the tight space. As we crawled, the sound of footsteps grew louder beneath us.

"I didn't think my first mission would involve me being a rat in a vent," I panted, pushing forward.

"I'm just hoping we don't encounter any actual rats," Nadia

replied in a hushed tone.

After what felt like an eternity, we saw a grate leading outside. With a collective push, we burst out of the facility, landing in a heap on the grass.

"Elegant exit," I said, laughing as I pulled Nadia to her feet.

"That was close," she replied, brushing dirt off her clothes.

Looking back at the hatch, now closed and innocuous once more, I took a deep breath. "We got what we came for, and we got out. It's a win in my book."

Nadia nodded, a smirk playing on her lips. "A win with a side of adrenaline. Now, about that coffee you mentioned earlier..."

Chuckling, I replied, "Only if you promise not to get us involved in any more squirrel-related incidents."

Nadia playfully rubbed her chin with an exaggerated, pensive expression. "No promises."

As we teleported to our safe rendezvous point, I couldn't help but think that if this was what being a demigod was all about, it was going to be one wild ride.

Reappearing at the north side of the forest felt like a breath of fresh air after the stifling tension of the facility. The sun had begun its ascent, casting the early morning glow across the vast expanse of green. Birds chirped overhead, and there was a stillness in the air, a stark contrast to the heart-pounding chase we'd just escaped.

"I could really use that coffee now," I groaned, stretching my stiff muscles.

Nadia nodded, still trying to catch her breath. "You and me both. I feel like I just ran a marathon."

We began to make our way to the local coffee shop I'd mentioned earlier. The freshly baked pastries and brewed coffee aroma greeted us long before we reached the entrance.

As we walked in, the bell above the door jingled, drawing the attention of the barista. A young lad, probably in his early twenties, with a mop of curly hair and glasses that seemed perpetually on the verge of sliding off his nose.

"Morning, ladies!" he greeted cheerfully. "What can I get for you?"

I ordered a caramel latte with whipped cream on top, while Nadia went for a black coffee with a dash of cinnamon.

"I'll never understand your taste," I commented, eyeing her drink.

Nadia just winked. "You'll learn to appreciate the finer things in life someday."

We found a cosy corner near the window and settled in. The sun's rays filtered through the glass, bathing our table in a warm glow. Despite the adrenaline rush and danger we'd faced, the moment felt strangely serene.

"You know," Nadia began, taking a sip of her coffee, "we really need to discuss our strategy for the next mission."

I sighed. "Can't we enjoy our victory coffee first?"

She chuckled. "Alright, alright. Five minutes. Then we strategize."

Five minutes turned into ten, then twenty, as we recounted our escapades from the academy days, laughing at our shared memories and antics. The world outside seemed to slow, our worries momentarily forgotten.

As we finally prepared to leave, the curly-haired barista approached our table. "Hey, I couldn't help but overhear some of your conversation. You guys are... bird-watchers, right?"

Nadia and I exchanged a glance, a smirk forming on our lips.

"Something like that," I replied, winking. "We're on a special kind of... ornithological assignment."

He grinned. "Well, if you ever need a local guide, I know this forest like the back of my hand. Name's Jamie."

"We'll keep that in mind, Jamie," Nadia replied, offering him a warm smile.

As we stepped outside, I turned to Nadia, a playful gleam in my eyes. "Bird-watching, huh? We might have just found our perfect cover."

Nadia laughed. "And who knows, maybe Jamie will prove useful in more ways than one."

As we moved further away from the coffee shop, I halted abruptly, causing Nadia to nearly collide with me. I turned to her with a baffled expression, realization dawning on me.

"Wait a sec, Nadia," I began, pointing back in the direction of the facility, "Why did we scramble through that narrow, dust-filled vent to get to the surface just to teleport? We could have teleported right out of that locked room in the facility!"

Nadia blinked for a moment, processing the question. Then, her face broke into a smirk, her eyes dancing with mischief. "Well, for one, where's the fun in that? And two, think about it. If we teleported from within, they would've been on high alert right away, realizing something supernatural was involved. The vent escape at least made them believe we had some human-level cunning to outsmart their security."

I raised an eyebrow, lips pursed in mock annoyance. "Or, you just wanted to see me squeeze through that tiny vent and hear me complain about it."

Nadia chuckled, nudging me playfully with her elbow. "You've got to admit, it made for a good story. Plus, your grumbling was entertaining."

I sighed theatrically. "All this for your entertainment, huh? Remind me again why I teamed up with you?"

She laughed, looping her arm through mine. "Because deep down, you love the thrill just as much as I do. And admit it, the vent adventure is going to be one for the books."

"I'll give you that," I conceded, shaking my head in amusement. "But next time, let's skip the vents and opt for a more direct route, okay?"

Nadia winked. "No promises."

Our laughter echoed through the forest, our spirits high despite the challenges we knew were on the horizon.

We strolled back to our rendezvous point, the weight of the mission momentarily forgotten. The world was full of surprises, and with Nadia by my side, I was ready to face them all.

Our adventures were just beginning.

Chapter 12

Ah, high school! A time for pimples, awkward first dates, and hormonal ups and downs. But if you're me, Sophie O'Sullivan, it's more like sprouting unimaginable powers overnight, fighting off godly entities, and awkwardly teleporting into the boys' locker room. Yep, that last one happened, and no, I'm not proud of it.

Being a teenager is a handful. But being a teenager with recently acquired demigod powers? It's a whole roller coaster inside a hurricane, with a hint of volcanic eruption on the side.

I remember one of the first 'incidents' when all this started. One day I was practising my free throws in the gym, and then **bam**, I sent the ball hurling with the force of a cannon, smashing the backboard. My gym teacher's face was a blend of amazement and fear, with a hint of "I'm not getting paid enough for this."

Then came the elemental surprises. I discovered that during emotional outbursts, the weather got… interesting. Like when Nadia beat me at video games, a small whirlwind appeared in my living room. Or when I got too excited watching a romantic movie and accidentally made it snow indoors. Romantic, right?

It wasn't just the elemental shifts. Teleportation seemed like an absolute win, in theory. But the reality? Let's just say there's a reason why you should visualize where you're teleporting clearly. I've found myself stuck halfway inside walls, on treetops, and, as previously mentioned, in places where teenage girls really shouldn't be.

And now, this new thing. Control over matter at a subatomic level. When Captain Hills mentioned it, I had a complete nerdgasm. I mean, isn't that something straight out of a sci-fi movie? But trust me, when you accidentally disintegrate your math textbook (or maybe that was on purpose?), the reality of such power starts sinking in.

I sat on the roof of the academy one night, looking at the stars, pondering my existential demigod dilemmas. A soft breeze rustled my hair, and a small cloud formed above me, sprinkling tiny raindrops. My elemental side was reacting to my pensive mood, I supposed.

"Thinking about the universe and your place in it?" A familiar voice chimed in. Nadia. She had this knack for turning up at the most opportune moments.

"More like wondering if I'll ever get a grip on these…abilities. Yesterday, I tried to pick up a spoon, and it turned into a fork!"

She laughed, "That's useful. I always seem to find spoons when I need forks."

I chuckled, "See, this is the problem! I want to be a fierce demigod with epic powers. Not a living, breathing kitchen appliance organizer."

She sat next to me. "You know, most of us go through our teenage years wishing we had something special about us. You've got it in spades. And sure, it's overwhelming and unpredictable. But it's also…incredible."

"Yeah, but most teenagers don't accidentally teleport into places they shouldn't or make it rain during a math test," I retorted.

She grinned, "Well, makes your high school memoir a hell of a lot more interesting than the rest of ours. Well, if we call the Academy a High-School…"

I laid back, staring at the vast expanse above. "I just…I wish there was a manual, you know? 'Demigod Powers for Dummies' or something."

Nadia lay down next to me. "That'd be one thick manual. But remember, you're evolving, Sophie. This isn't the Ancient Race's plan gone wrong. This is something new, something no one's seen before. And while it's chaotic and confusing, it's also groundbreaking."

I turned to her, "When did you become so philosophical?"

She shrugged, "Around the same time my friend started turning spoons into forks."

We both laughed and momentarily felt the weight of my unprecedented transformation feel lighter.

"I guess it's just…growing pains," I murmured. "Super-charged, demigod-style growing pains."

Nadia nudged me, "And you're not alone. Remember that. For every spoon you turn into a fork, every accidental rain cloud, every mis-teleportation, you've got people who've got your back."

I smiled, feeling a warmth that had nothing to do with my elemental powers. "Thanks, Nad. That means a lot."

"Anytime," she said. "Now, how about you make it snow? I could use some winter vibes."

I chuckled, "Only if you promise not to start a snowball fight."

She smirked, "No promises."

And as the first flake floated down, for the first time in a long while, I felt content in my unpredictable, chaotic, utterly unique journey of self-discovery.

The night wore on, with the moon's soft glow as our primary light source. Snowflakes gently blanketed the academy rooftop. I cherished moments like this - an escape from the constant chaos of my new life.

After a few minutes of peaceful snow-watching, Nadia broke the silence, "You ever thought of creating something, you know, instead of just turning spoons into forks?"

"Like what?" I asked, intrigued by the thought.

She drew a circle in the snow, "Like, say, turning this into a pizza?"

I laughed, "I've not tried making food appear out of thin air. But with my control over matter at a subatomic level, I guess I might eventually get there?"

"Great! Let's start with the basics then. How about you try creating, I don't know, a snowball?"

I shot her a suspicious look, "You just want to start that snowball fight, don't you?"

She feigned innocence, "Who, me? Never."

But I humoured her, concentrating hard on a patch of snow, trying to will it into a compact ball. To my amazement and Nadia's delight, a perfectly round snowball formed in my palm.

Nadia applauded, "Look at you, elemental snowball-maker extraordinaire!"

I beamed, "It's all in a day's work."

No sooner had I said that, Nadia grabbed the snowball and threw it at me. I ducked, and it hit the door of the stairwell.

"Hey! No fair!" I protested, quickly making another snowball and hurling it at her.

What started as an introspective evening quickly turned into an all-out snowball war. It was as if the universe was reminding me that amid all the newfound powers and responsibilities, I was still a teenager, and there was always time for some fun.

Finally, breathless and covered in snow, we called a truce.

"You're quite the opponent, O'Sullivan," Nadia said, brushing snow out of her hair.

"Right back at you, Rostov."

We lay back, once again staring at the moonlit sky. The snow had stopped, but the rooftop was now covered in a shimmering white blanket.

"I know it's a lot," Nadia began, her voice soft, "All these changes, the unexpected turns your life has taken. But you're handling it with grace, even if you don't see it. Sure, there are hiccups, like the occasional fork instead of a spoon, but you're growing. Evolving."

I sighed, "It just feels like I'm forever playing catch up. Just when I think I've gotten a handle on one power, another one pops up."

"But that's the beauty of it, isn't it?" Nadia mused, "You're not stagnant. You're constantly moving, learning, and evolving. It's like life, unpredictable and ever-changing."

"And full of snowball fights?" I quipped.

She laughed, "Especially full of snowball fights."

As the night turned into the early hours of morning, I felt grateful. Grateful for the powers, no matter how unpredictable they were. Grateful for friends like Nadia, who reminded me of the silver lining in every cloud or snowstorm. And most of all, grateful for the journey - the wild, unexpected, roller-coaster journey of self-discovery. The life of a demigod teenager was anything but ordinary, but then again, who wanted ordinary?

* * *

And as I was still savouring that sensation, a familiar voice rang in my head.

"Hey, girl! I see you are coping quite well with your new situation. I'm impressed!"

Phoebe!

"Show yourself, Phoebe!" I said. "You know I prefer to see you when we talk!"

In a flash of shimmering light, Phoebe materialized before me. Unlike the legends that portrayed her as a radiant goddess with flowing garments, Phoebe stood before me wearing modern jeans, a leather jacket, and the most amusing pair of sneakers that glowed in the dark.

"Oh, come on, Soph," Phoebe said with a smirk, admiring her shoes. "Just because I'm ancient doesn't mean I can't keep up with the fashion trends. These are the latest. What do you think?"

I chuckled, "They're… illuminating. But seriously, the Ancient Titaness of prophecy and intellect wears glowing sneakers now? What's next? Selfie sessions at the Olympus gym?"

Phoebe did a mock gasp. "Don't give me ideas! But now that you mention it, I think I'd totally rock the gym selfies."

I laughed. "No doubt. You were always the cool, quirky one, even among the ancients."

She winked, tossing her hair dramatically. "Guilty as charged. But back to business: How's the demigod life treating you? Any side effects from the unexpected DNA tweaks?"

"Well, besides turning spoons into forks and teleporting into closets accidentally, I'm managing just fine," I replied with a playful grin.

"Oh, the usual teenage demigod problems then. I remember

when I first tried to master my powers. Ended up turning the entire night sky into a disco ball. You should've seen Zeus's face!" Phoebe chuckled, reminiscing.

"That must have been one 'lit' night!" I giggled. "Anyway, to what do I owe the pleasure of this visit?"

Phoebe leaned in conspiratorially. "Just checking in on my star recruit, making sure you're not wreaking too much havoc. I heard about the Shakespeare-reciting rabbit."

I blushed, "That was…creative, wasn't it?"

"Creative? It's legendary! You might have given me competition in the fun department." Phoebe praised with a wink.

We both burst out laughing, the sound echoing around us.

After catching her breath, Phoebe looked at me earnestly, "But on a serious note, Soph, you're doing great. Everyone has their bumps along the way, and given the unpredictability of your powers, you're handling it like a champ."

"Thanks, Phoebe. That means a lot, coming from you."

She hugged me briefly. "Always here for you, girl. And remember, if things get too tough, just call on me. We'll have a girls' night out—goddess style."

I chuckled, imagining the mischief we could create, "I'll keep that in mind. And, hey, if I ever need fashion advice, especially about glowing sneakers, I know who to call."

As Phoebe began to fade away, she left me with a wink and her trademark radiant smile, "Stay fabulous, Soph!"

And with a flash of light, she was gone. I shook my head with a chuckle, grateful for her impromptu visit. No matter how challenging things got, it was comforting to know I had a Titaness on speed dial.

Chapter 13

This morning, I will experience a new first-timer: the mission execution briefing. Nadia and I worked on a slide presentation all morning, but conscious that this time was a real report, not the usual exercise.

"Ready?" Nadia asked when we reached the conference room door.

"No." I said, "But here goes nothing." And I opened the door and led the way in.

Captain Hills was waiting for us, sitting at the large oval table. Another person was on her side. I had never seen him before. He was an important figure, looking about 40 on my human scale—dark hair, wearing a tactical jumpsuit.

"Good morning, girls," said Hill. "Thank you for being on time. This is Lt. Colonel Marco Mariani from the regional strategic command."

"Sir!" Nadia and I said almost at once.

A superior officer from the regional command was here? This will make our first report a real hell. Nadia and I looked at each other, sharing a sense of unease that was clouding my brain.

"At ease, agents. I don't bite!" Said Mariani. "I can hear your teeth grinding from here! We are military, but we try to keep formalism to the bare minimum, so please relax. As I said, I don't bite!"

"Not usually!" added Hills with a wink.

"Okay, we'll try to keep this report within the 'usual' then!" I said, attempting a smile while taking my seat and connecting the laptop to the presentation screen.

"Get started, agents," Mariani said.

I started the briefing from our arrival, skipping Nadia's need for caffeine. I tried to stick to the 2-minute-per-slide rule, but it was hard. Nadia and I presented different sections of the slides' deck, trying to be as concise and professional as we could, but elements such as the animal diversion didn't call for seriousness, so we both couldn't avoid some puns.

" A bespectacled rabbit reciting Shakespeare?" asked Mariani with a bemused expression. "I give you that you are creative agents! And I suppose you dismissed the 'old lady', correct? I don't see anything about her in your report. Her reaction was not a normal human reaction to the show you started, and you didn't consider that any suspicious?"

I froze. Nadia went pale. How could we have missed that detail? That lady was likely one of the Ancient Race.

"Erm, I suppose we just assumed she was an odd old lady thinking we were working on some carnival show, Sir," Nadia said.

"You 'assumed'? Do I really have to remind you of the old saying about 'ASS-U-ME'?" Mariani asked, not amused at all. "You kept going without even stopping to ask yourselves who that lady was and what risk she could have presented to you. Are you two fucking kidding me?"

"No, Sir! We see it now, Sir!" I said. "We did make a mistake in judgement, Sir."

"A mistake?" Captain Hills said. "That was a titanic screw-up, that it was! You could have been killed on the spot. You two dickheads! You just fucked up a simple recon mission, statistically getting killed!"

Nadia and I felt so small and embarrassed, like two total screw-ups that just failed the most important event of their lives. Hills and Mariani were now standing, their faces covered in palpable anger, eyes fixed on us.

Not a sound now in the room. Nadia and I with our eyes on the floor. the silence was almost unbearable.

Then, the door slammed open, startling us. In the silence we were imbued a moment before that door felt like an explosion.

And there entered the old lady from the forest, notebook in hand, smiling. Her appearance slowly changed while she walked toward the table, getting younger at every step. Joining us at the table was a woman in her 40s, now grinning at us.

"Agents-screw-ups, let me introduce you to Metis, one of our most cunning operatives. You might remember her from history classes as the first wife of our leader, Zeus," Hills said, grinning.

Mariani took a step back, allowing Metis to occupy the room's attention. "Good work on the camouflage, Metis," he remarked.

Metis curtsied, the grin never leaving her face. "It's an art, really. The… rabbit quite entertained me," she said, suppressing a chuckle.

"Wait, so you weren't…?" I began, trying to put the pieces together.

"An actual oblivious old lady? No, dear. I was sent to evaluate how well you'd perform," Metis replied. "Although I must admit, you had me convinced for a bit with the rabbit."

Nadia shifted uncomfortably in her seat. "So, we were being tested the whole time?"

Captain Hills nodded, amusement dancing in her eyes. "While it wasn't the primary purpose, the secondary was to test how observant and adaptable you'd be. It wasn't entirely a recon mission, per se. It was also an evaluation."

Metis leaned back in her chair, surveying us. "And while you had some excellent moments, you had… others that were less than stellar. For instance, dismissing me."

Nadia and I exchanged another look, this time one of embarrassment. It was one thing to mess up and another to realize we'd been bested by someone watching our every move and every misstep.

I cleared my throat. "So, this means we failed the mission?"

Captain Hills leaned forward, resting her elbows on the table. "No, not completely. You gathered intel, executed several tactics correctly, and made it back with valuable information. But there were slip-ups, moments of inattention that could be fatal in a real-world scenario."

Metis interjected, "In your defence, the two of you are fresh from the academy. Real missions have unpredictable variables. You learn from each experience, adapt, and improve."

Nadia sighed, "I guess we were just so excited about our first mission that we lost sight of the details."

Metis smiled sympathetically. "That happens, even to the best. The key is not letting it deter you. Learning from your mistakes is what will shape you into better agents."

Trying to inject some humour into the heavy atmosphere, I joked, "So next time, we're going to be wary of every old lady?"

Captain Hills chuckled, "Not just old ladies. Be suspicious of everyone and everything. But also, balance it with common sense."

Mariani nodded, "Paranoia isn't a strategy, it's a reaction. We want you to be strategic in your thinking, always a step ahead."

There was a momentary pause, and then Metis leaned forward, looking directly into our eyes. "You know, the world of espionage and recon isn't about being flawless. It's about being adaptable. Sometimes, you'll face rabbits reciting poetry, and sometimes ancient goddesses disguised as old ladies. The question isn't how you missed it; it's how you adapt and learn from it."

I looked over at Nadia, taking strength from her presence. "We appreciate the feedback. And we will definitely learn from it."

Nadia added, "No more mistaking goddesses for old ladies, for starters."

The room filled with laughter, a sign of the tension lifting.

Captain Hills stood, signalling the end of the briefing. "You're dismissed. Reflect on this, and come back better. And remember, every mission is an opportunity to learn."

As Nadia and I exited the room, I whispered, "Who knew the world of demigods would be filled with such sneaky tests?"

She smirked, "Makes you wonder what's waiting for us next, doesn't it?"

I grinned, "Bring it on."

The world of gods, agents, and espionage was unpredictable, but we were becoming sharper, wiser, and ready for the next challenge with each hurdle.

III

Part Three

Chapter 14

A knock on the door woke me up. An insistent knocking, I must add. That interrupted my Sunday afternoon beauty nap. Not cool. I went for the door and opened it with my best WTFYW face.

A cadet was there, standing, holding an envelope. My face made him feel bad, and I felt terrible for that… for a fraction of a second.

"What is this, cadet?" I asked.

"It's from Captain Hills, Sir," he said. "The captain is asking for you to join her in the first briefing room on the third floor, Sir."

"Sir? Me? do I look that old to you, cadet?" I said, feigning being offended. His face was priceless. He started bubbling some "Sorry, Madam", giving me a better opportunity to keep the joke going. "Madam, now? Really, cadet?"

He stammered, "Uh, Miss? Lady? Um… Sophie?"

"Ah! Finally, you get it right," I chuckled, "Just Sophie will do. And don't worry, my face could kill if looks were lethal, but I'm quite harmless. Well, unless you interrupt my naps again."

His nervous chuckles merged with mine, and he awkwardly shifted from one foot to the other, "I'll remember that. The nap part, especially Sophie."

"Good. So, Captain Hills sent you, huh?" I said, tapping the envelope. "Anything you can share about what's in here?"

He shrugged, a sheepish grin playing on his lips. "Sorry, just the messenger here. All I know is that she said it was urgent."

I gave an exaggerated sigh. "Of course, it's urgent. Probably wants to discuss the last mission, or maybe she's bored and wants company. Or perhaps, just maybe, she's heard of my impeccable taste in shoes and wants fashion advice." I wiggled my eyebrows humorously.

The cadet's lips quirked up into a half-smile. "I wouldn't be surprised. Those shoes are… unique."

"They're the pinnacle of style, my dear cadet. But I guess we'll just have to see what this 'urgent' matter is all about."

"Indeed, Sophie," he replied with a more relaxed air. "Anyway, best not to keep the captain waiting."

I winked at him. "Thanks for the message, and don't worry next time, I'll make sure to hang a 'Do Not Disturb' sign on my door."

"That might be wise," he chuckled, giving a mock salute before heading down the hallway.

Shaking my head in amusement, I quickly grabbed my jacket and headed out. Whatever Captain Hills wanted, it was bound to be an adventure. And as always, I was up for the ride.

I paused mid-stride, curiosity gnawing at me. The corridor was empty, the sounds of the Academy a faint buzz in the distance. Using the quiet moment, I decided to sneak a peek inside the envelope. With a swift motion, I pulled out the contents: two photos.

The first photo showcased a vast landscape; from the topography and vegetation, I immediately recognized it as somewhere in Queensland, Australia. There was something peculiar about it. Nothing overtly stood out, but knowing Captain Hills, there would be a specific reason why I was being shown a seemingly ordinary satellite shot of the Australian wilderness.

The next photo nearly made me stop dead in my tracks. It was of a man with a cold, emotionless stare. The chilling look in his eyes was enough to make my skin crawl. But what really caught my attention was the bold annotation at the bottom: "Deimos - threat level: very high."

Deimos? As in, the Ancient Greek deity of terror? Oh boy. This was either a terrible code name, or things were about to get a whole lot more complicated. And honestly, with my recent track record, I wouldn't be surprised if the universe was throwing a legit Greek deity my way. As if being a newly minted demigod wasn't enough, right?

I pondered over the two images. What did a remote location in Queensland have to do with this Deimos character? And why was I being looped into this?

Mulling over the possible connections, I slid the photos back into the envelope. My leisurely stroll became a brisk walk. Clearly, this wasn't just a casual meet-up with Captain Hills; something big was unfolding.

I reached the third floor, making a beeline for the first briefing room. The gravity of the situation weighed heavily on me, but if there was anything I had learned so far in the Academy, it was that humour was my shield and wit, my sword. Whatever Captain Hills had in store, Deimos or not, I was ready to face it.

Grasping the handle of the briefing room door, I took a deep breath, mentally preparing myself. With a swift push, I entered the room, holding the envelope tightly in my hand. I hoped the Academy had prepared me enough to face whatever was on the horizon.

* * *

In the briefing room, I found Hills and Mariani waiting. Nadia arrived while I was closing the door, almost on her face. We looked at each other, exchanging a meaningful look of excitement and fear.

"Sorry for interrupting your Sunday nap, Sophie," Hills said with a smirk.

"Does everybody know about my napping habits?" I asked, feigning a stupor.

Nadia and I took our places at the table, and Mariani started the debriefing, Deimos' picture on the holographic screen.

"Our intelligence has confirmed the location of Deimos' training facility for his personal demigod. All we know is that he has selected a human, just like our Phoebe selected Sophie here," Mariani said.

"We know that this new demigod will have one single goal: provoke instability and war among humans."

"Deimos want to reclaim the status of 'Gods' to our race, and he's willing to go to extreme measures to achieve his objective."

"Your mission is to identify this human and evaluate his threat level."

Mariani paused, letting the weight of the information sink in. The room was silent, the soft humming of the holo-projector the only noise in the background.

"So… you're saying there's another me out there? Only evil? " I quipped, raising an eyebrow.

"Seems that way," Nadia mused, "only he probably doesn't

nap on Sundays." She shot me a cheeky grin.

I rolled my eyes at her remark but couldn't help a small chuckle. "Everyone needs their beauty sleep, Nadia."

"I knew about this from Phoebe's initial recruiting pitch, but then nothing about this ever came up again," I said. "I guess my naps are going to suffer a serious cut if this pans out."

Mariani coughed to regain our attention. "Deimos isn't known for playing nice, ladies. He's been around the block and is well aware of the power a demigod can wield. That's why he's looking to create one in his own image."

Hills leaned forward. "To make matters more interesting, our intel suggests that the chosen human is already undergoing the transformation process. They're rapidly gaining abilities and powers."

I leaned back in my chair, digesting the information. "So, essentially, we're looking at a high-speed, potentially unstable demigod-in-making with world-ending goals. How's that for a Monday morning briefing?"

Nadia nudged me. "It's Sunday evening, genius."

"Oh, right," I replied sheepishly.

Hills took a moment to continue. "This mission is about strategy, subtlety, and discernment. Not brute force. Deimos might know about Sophie's capabilities, but he doesn't know she's coming."

Mariani added, "What makes it trickier is the location of the facility. It's situated in the heart of Queensland's tropical rainforests. Remote, off-grid, shielded from most surveillance tools we have. That's where the satellite image comes in."

He gestured towards the holographic screen, switching the display to the satellite image I had seen earlier. "This, agents, is where we believe the facility is located. But you won't be able to just teleport in. The place is covered with a unique energy barrier that disrupts teleportation."

I groaned. "So, what? We're going to hike through the Aussie outback, avoiding kangaroos and koalas, just to sneak up on Deimos' lair?"

Nadia smirked, "Sounds fun, doesn't it? A real adventure!"

Hills glared at us. "This isn't a joke, agents. That forest is home to a number of dangerous creatures, both normal and... other. And I'm not just talking about spiders or snakes."

My imagination ran wild. Were we talking about mutant kangaroos? Giant koalas? Flying wombats?

"Like what?" Nadia's voice brought me back to the present.

"Rumors say that there are creatures there loyal to Deimos. Beings that have been enhanced and twisted to serve his purpose," Mariani explained.

"Great, just what we needed," I sighed. "Evil forest minions."

Hills interjected, "Deimos' objective is more than just personal ambition. He wants to stir chaos, shift power dynamics, and make himself indispensable to the Ancients. If he can set the world aflame with his demigod, the Ancients might just turn to him as their saviour. It's a risky plan, but it just might work."

Nadia frowned, "We can't let that happen. What's our timeframe?"

Mariani replied, "We believe the transformation will be complete in a matter of weeks. It's a tight window, but we need to move swiftly."

I tapped the satellite image, "What's the plan?"

"We need to gather more intel. Observe the facility, assess the situation, and find the human before the transformation completes," Hills said. "Once we have that, we can plan our next steps."

Mariani nodded, "Discretion is key. Deimos cannot know we're onto him until we're ready to act."

I leaned in, feeling the gravity of the situation. "We'll need gear, intel on the area, local contacts, maybe some Aussie slang lessons. When do we start?"

Hills grinned, "Immediately. Get prepped, and meet me at the teleportation chamber in three hours."

As Nadia and I left the room, I leaned in and whispered, "This mission might just be our biggest challenge yet."

She chuckled, "I just hope there's good coffee in Queensland."

Chapter 15

In the dimly lit chamber of the council, Mariani, Hills, Phoebe, and Metis gathered around an intricately carved round table. The table bore markings of the Ancient Race's history, but today's discussion was focused on the future, on a certain human-turned-nearly-Ancient.

Mariani spread a DNA multi-helix hologram in the centre. It was shimmering and fluid, with various colours indicating the multiple changes. "Ladies and gentlemen, behold the ever-evolving DNA of Sophie. Honestly, it reminds me of a disco in the 80s."

Hills squinted at it. "Do you mean its complex structure or its ability to surprise us at every twist and turn?"

"Both," Mariani chuckled. "Every time we think we've got a grip on it, Sophie throws us another curveball."

Phoebe leaned forward, her ethereal aura contrasting with the high-tech visuals. "In my time, we used our wisdom to shape the destinies of select humans. Buddha, Jesus, and others. Simple nudges to guide humanity. It seems we've not just nudged with Sophie but shoved her down a cosmic slide of rapid evolution."

Metis smirked, "Trust you always to overachieve, Phoebe."

Phoebe rolled her eyes, "Oh please, like you weren't the

overachiever who tried tricking Zeus."

Metis chuckled, "Ancient history, my dear. But back to Sophie. Are we...prepared for this?"

Hills shook her head, "We aimed for a few powers, some simple enhancements. But she's breaking every mould we had. She's not just a 'messenger'; she's becoming one of us."

Mariani sighed, "The real question is, why? What's so different this time?"

Phoebe pondered, "The world's different. More interconnected. Could the global consciousness be accelerating her evolution?"

Metis mused, "Or maybe it's just teenage hormones."

Hills chuckled, "I doubt 'teenage hormones' can rewrite DNA to this extent."

Metis smirked, "You'd be surprised. Remember the time when Zeus turned into a swan? I blame his teenage years."

The room echoed with laughter. However, Mariani sobered first, "Humor aside, we need to discuss this with the High Council. We are treading unknown waters, and they need to be prepared for any eventuality."

Phoebe nodded, "But how do we approach it? They've always been... traditional. This level of DNA manipulation is unprecedented."

Metis leaned in, "We present it as it is. A marvel of evolution. A new chapter in our history. This isn't just about Sophie; it's about us and our legacy."

Hills agreed, "We should monitor her closely but also guide her. If she truly is evolving into an Ancient, she'd need our wisdom and support."

Mariani paused, "And if she surpasses us? Becomes something...more?"

Phoebe's eyes twinkled, "Then we celebrate. For in Sophie, our hopes for a better future might just be realized."

Metis raised an eyebrow, "Always the optimist. But she has a point. Maybe Sophie's evolution is what we've been waiting for. An envoy between two worlds."

Mariani nodded, "Let's prepare our case for the High Council. They need to see the potential, the hope, and not just the unpredictability."

As they started discussing the strategies, Hills paused, "And in the meantime, maybe someone should introduce Sophie to some responsibilities?"

Metis grinned, "Like paying rent?"

Phoebe chuckled, "Maybe not that cruel."

The room filled with light laughter, knowing well that the path ahead was uncertain, but the journey was sure to be interesting.

The council chamber echoed with their laughter, the kind that comes from centuries of camaraderie. But the gravity of the situation wasn't lost on them.

Mariani, sifting through some papers, noted, "Let's consider some hypothetical scenarios. If Sophie does fully transition to an Ancient, how do we integrate her into our world without overwhelming her?"

Metis quipped, "We could start by inviting her to our monthly potluck. Maybe she has some human recipes to share."

Phoebe, amused, responded, "The last time we tried 'human cuisine', Mariani had heartburn for a week."

Mariani chuckled, "Those spicy tacos were a mistake. But in all seriousness, her evolution is faster than anything we've seen. We need to ensure her mental and emotional state remains stable."

Hills pondered, "Maybe she needs a mentor. Someone who's been through the process, albeit much slower."

Phoebe's eyes twinkled, "Are you volunteering, Metis?"

Metis smirked, "Oh no, I've had my fair share of mentoring. Zeus was a handful. But perhaps she needs someone relatable, someone closer to her age, or at least appears to be."

Hills mused, "Someone to be her guide, her confidante. A bridge between her human past and her Ancient future."

Mariani added, "Yes, but it also needs to be someone who can reign her in if things go south. Her powers are vast and still evolving. We can't predict what she might manifest next."

Phoebe sighed, "The unpredictability is both a wonder and a concern. But remember, we're not just dealing with a set of powers; we're dealing with a young girl. She needs support, understanding, and a lot of patience."

Metis grinned, "Oh, the joys of adolescence combined with god-like powers. What could possibly go wrong?"

Hills playfully nudged Metis, "Always the joker. But you're not wrong. We need to approach this delicately."

Mariani chimed in, "Our mission is twofold. Firstly, to understand the cause and extent of her rapid evolution. And secondly, to guide her through this tumultuous phase. Remember, she's still largely human in her emotions and experiences."

Phoebe added, "Which makes her unique. She's a blend of human vulnerability and Ancient capability. This combination might just be what we need to bridge our world with theirs."

Metis teased, "So, Phoebe, any regrets in choosing Sophie?"

Phoebe smiled warmly, "Not for a moment. Every twist, turn, and surprise she throws our way only reinforces my belief that she's special."

Hills concluded, "Then it's settled. We'll present the case to the High Council, highlighting Sophie's potential. Meanwhile, we find her a mentor, someone to guide her. And Metis, maybe you could tone down on the teasing. We don't want her turning you into a frog or something."

Metis winked, "I always fancied being an amphibian."

The chamber resonated with their laughter once more, but beneath it all was a sense of purpose. The journey with Sophie had only just begun, and they were determined to see it through.

Chapter 16

The entire teleportation chamber was a marvel of Ancient technology – a swirling blend of both magic and machine. The walls pulsated gently, humming their low-frequency tune like a chorus of cosmic whales. Swirls of blue light painted the room, moving as if they were sentient, curiously inspecting those who dared to harness their power.

Hills stood steadfast amidst the ambience, her usually confident stature tinged with a hint of vulnerability. The fingers on her right hand unconsciously tapped away against her thigh. I knew this rhythmic drumming all too well – it was her signature tell when she was worried.

Catching her gesture, I decided to inject some levity. "Captain, is that the secret Ancient Morse code, or are you hinting at a hidden musical talent?"

Hills looked momentarily taken aback, then chuckled softly. "Perhaps a bit of both. But I'll have you know, Sophie, the last time I exhibited my 'musical talent,' we lost three recruits to the dance floor."

Laughing, I quipped, "Oh, that sounds dangerously entertaining!"

Nadia, who had just entered the chamber, glanced between us, an eyebrow arched inquisitively. "Did I just walk into a talent show audition?"

"Just discussing the Captain's secret dance techniques," I replied, giving Nadia a sly grin.

Hills shot me a faux stern look, "A captain never reveals her secrets. But trust me, they're legendary."

Nadia smirked, "Now that's a show I'd pay to see."

But our jesting was soon interrupted as the chamber's ambient lights shifted from their calming blue to an urgent amber hue. The machinery began its gentle whirring, indicating the onset of the teleportation sequence.

Hills, once again the epitome of professionalism, addressed us, "As much as I'd love to continue our comedy hour, remember, we've got a mission. I trust you both, but Deimos is cunning. Always be on your toes."

"We've got this, Captain," Nadia said confidently, flashing her freshly polished nails. "See this shade? It's called 'Distract and Conquer.'"

I squinted playfully at the glittery hue, "Is that our secret strategy then?"

Nadia winked, "Absolutely! If all else fails, I'll just dazzle them with sparkles."

"And if that doesn't work," I added with feigned seriousness, "I'll deploy my secret weapon – unparalleled teenage drama. No one can resist its chaotic allure."

Hills laughed, a hearty sound that echoed in the chamber. "You two have a knack for making everything seem less daunting. But seriously, stay alert. Deimos might not be easily swayed by nail polish or drama."

Nadia saluted cheekily, "Understood, Captain Shimmershake."

Hills rolled her eyes, a playful smile tugging at her lips.

"Prepare yourselves."

The room surged with energy, the colours becoming blindingly intense. The familiar disorienting sensation of teleportation enveloped us – a feeling akin to being stretched through the vast cosmos and then snapped back together.

Hills' voice pierced through the disarray, a grounding force amidst the chaos. "Return safely, both of you."

And just like that, we were catapulted into the unknown.

*　*　*

With an anticlimactic thud, we found ourselves on the sandy shores of Wonga Beach, the brisk salty breeze tugging at our hair. The vast expanse of the Coral Sea stretched infinitely on one side, while the dense greenery of the Daintree Rainforest beckoned from the other.

"Really? The teleportation chamber again?" Nadia grumbled, wiping away a smear of sand from her cheek. "We could have just teleported ourselves directly into the forest, you know."

I raised an eyebrow, giving her a sly grin. "What, and miss out on this lovely seaside view? Besides, think of all the steps we'll add to our fitness trackers."

Nadia rolled her eyes but couldn't hide her smirk. "My tracker is still recovering from our last mission; thank you very much."

I chuckled. "Remember, we're supposed to be tourists!"

She looked down at our attire – hiking boots, khaki shorts, and shirts layered with more equipment than most small armies carry. "Speaking of looking like tourists... I'm pretty sure no regular tourist carries this much stuff."

I smirked, holding up a waterproof pouch. "You never know

when you'll need an underwater flashlight, a foldable tent, or an emergency snack."

"You mean chocolate."

I winked. "Always be prepared!"

As we began our trek toward the heart of the rainforest, the sounds of waves crashing behind us gradually gave way to the orchestra of the forest. Birds chirped melodiously from the canopy, unseen insects buzzed, and every so often, a distant rustle hinted at the multitude of creatures going about their business.

The rainforest was a cacophony of colours and scents. The air was thick with humidity and the rich, earthy aroma of decaying leaves. Trees with massive roots rose high, their canopies filtering the sunlight and casting the forest floor in a greenish hue. Every now and then, we'd catch a glimpse of a vibrant bird taking flight or a colourful butterfly flitting by.

"Gosh, it's so hot and humid," Nadia complained, swiping at her forehead. "And I swear, these mosquitoes have a personal vendetta against me."

"You know," I began with feigned casualness, "if you controlled your temperature the way I do—"

"Don't even start, Miss Elemental Powers," she interrupted with mock irritation. "Some of us prefer the good old-fashioned method of complaining."

I grinned. "Just offering a solution!"

We continued deeper into the forest, the dense foliage occasionally giving way to beautiful clearings. In one such opening, a serene stream danced over pebbles, its water so clear we could see small fish darting about.

Nadia paused, tilting her head. "You hear that?"

"What? The enchanting sounds of nature?"

"No… That." She pointed ahead where faint sounds of chatter were discernible.

"Oh, right. Humans. I sometimes forget about them."

"Because you're so elevated?" Nadia teased.

"Exactly. Now come on, we have to blend in."

As we approached, we spotted a group of tourists guided by a local, pointing out various flora and fauna. We joined the back, pretending to be engrossed.

After a while, Nadia leaned in, whispering, "Ever feel like we're in one of those nature documentaries?"

I snorted. "Every. Single. Time. I half expect someone to commentate our every move."

"'And here, we have the elusive Sophie, known for her innate ability to attract mischief…'" Nadia narrated in a deep, dramatic tone.

I giggled, "'And next to her, the rare Nadia, with her unparalleled talent for walking into prickly things.'"

"Hey! That was one time!"

We both laughed, drawing curious looks from the others. With an innocent smile, I said, "Just so amazed by nature."

And thus, amidst the thick foliage, vibrant wildlife, and under the canopy of the ancient Daintree Rainforest, the duo continued their quest, blending in, bantering, and forever on the lookout for the unexpected.

* * *

The sun had begun its descent, casting long shadows and bathing the dense canopy in a soft golden hue. Despite the captivating beauty of the rainforest, the weight of our mission grew heavier with each step we took. And then, as we ventured further, an almost imperceptible hum met our ears. It wasn't the hum of nature; it was something else—something foreign. As if the air itself had thickened, we suddenly felt an invisible force field.

Nadia stopped, her eyes widening in recognition. "The protective magic field," she whispered.

I nodded in agreement, feeling the palpable energy around us. "Seems we've reached Deimos' front door."

We looked at each other, a shared understanding passing between us. While our banter and jokes had kept our spirits up, it was clear that now was the time to be deadly serious. Yet, even in the thick of it, Nadia couldn't help but whisper a quip, "Well, he's certainly not into doorbells, is he?"

I smirked. "Or welcome mats."

Adjusting our equipment and tightening the straps of our packs, we began to move forward, cautiously and deliberately, every step measured. Our senses were heightened. Every rustle in the bush, every call of a bird felt magnified.

Walking alongside Nadia, I felt a rush of gratitude for her presence. We had each other's backs, and that assurance was invaluable. "Remember," I whispered, "our first task is reconnaissance. We need to find the demigod and get a sense of the layout. Direct confrontations are our last resort."

Nadia simply nodded, her usual playful demeanour replaced by the cool, focused expression of a seasoned professional.

The deeper we went, the darker the surroundings became. Trees, older than time itself, blocked out most of the sunlight. Moss-covered trunks and vines snaked around our path, and the air grew cold and damp.

"Feels like we're not just battling Deimos but the very essence of this forest," Nadia remarked, her voice barely above a whisper.

"You're not entirely wrong," I replied. "The forest has its magic, its energy. And Deimos has tapped into it. The natural defences of the rainforest are now working in tandem with his dark magic."

The terrain grew rougher, and we found ourselves navigating tricky slopes and dense underbrush. At one point, we had to wade through a narrow stream, the water eerily still.

"I don't know about you," Nadia whispered as she sidestepped a suspiciously wobbly rock, "but I'm getting the feeling we're being watched."

I nodded. "Been feeling it since we entered this field. Eyes everywhere. Just can't pinpoint where."

We continued in this manner for what felt like hours, the weight of the forest's gaze never leaving us. Every now and then, we'd spot strange symbols etched onto tree trunks or rocks, each glowing faintly—a sure sign of Deimos' magic.

"This one looks like... a jellybean?" Nadia whispered, pointing at one such symbol.

I squinted. "No, more like an amoeba. Or... a weird blob? Either Deimos has a toddler drawing his symbols, or we're seriously missing something here."

We both chuckled softly but were promptly reminded of our mission when a chilling howl echoed through the trees.

Nadia grabbed my arm glancing around, her grip firm. "What the hell was that?"

"Not sure," I responded, straining my ears. "But it came from that direction," I pointed slightly to the northeast. "Towards the heart of the rainforest. That's where we need to go."

The path ahead was steep, but we pushed on, driven by determination and the need to uncover the secrets that the forest hid. As we moved closer to the source of the sound, a clearing emerged, revealing a massive stone temple, half-concealed by the forest's growth. Torches flamed at its entrance, and shadows flitted about, hinting at guards or perhaps other creatures.

I turned to Nadia, our strategy clear. "We'll circle around, find a vantage point. Understand what we're up against."

"Stay close, stay quiet," Nadia whispered back, her expression fierce.

My heart raced, not just from the exertion but also from the thrill of the mission. The game had indeed become real, and we were right in the thick of it.

The temple's massive stone walls looked ancient, weathered by time, and intertwined with the very fabric of the forest. It wasn't just built here; it felt like it had grown from the land itself. We approached with stealth, ensuring our footfalls were silent, blending our movements with the natural sounds of the forest.

Our first task was to find a high vantage point, so we circled the temple, searching for an accessible but discreet route upwards. Not too far from where we stood, a massive strangler fig wrapped its massive tendrils around the structure, its sprawling network of roots and branches offering a potential path upwards.

I motioned towards it. "Looks like nature's staircase."

"Just hope it doesn't decide to… strangle us," Nadia whispered back with a smirk, trying to lighten the tense mood.

Gently and cautiously, we began our ascent. The fig's gnarled roots provided decent footholds, and soon, we found ourselves high above the temple grounds. From our newfound height, the temple's design was clearer – a sprawling compound with various chambers, each potentially housing its secrets and dangers.

At the heart of the temple was a central courtyard, and from our vantage point, we could see a group gathered there. They surrounded a figure tied to a stone pillar. From a distance, it was hard to make out the details, but the scene had all the hallmarks of a ritual of some kind.

"Look," I whispered, pointing to the man tied up. "Could he be the human Deimos selected?"

Nadia peered closer, her brow furrowing. "It's hard to tell from here. But if it is him, we must get closer, understand what they're planning."

"Agreed," I replied. "But we need to be careful. This feels… bigger than just Deimos and his ambitions. This temple, the ritual – there's more at play here."

As we observed, the gathered group began to chant in a language that was unfamiliar, their voices rising and falling in a rhythm that sent shivers down our spines. The torches flared, the fire's dance becoming more frenzied.

"Sophie," Nadia's voice trembled slightly, "do you feel that?"

I nodded, feeling a surge of power emanating from the temple. "Deimos is drawing from ancient magic. Whatever he's planning, it's beginning."

Our eyes locked. The weight of the situation settled in, but there was also a silent resolve. We were here for a reason, and the odds stacked against us wouldn't deter our mission. This was no game. Not only is this reality, but a matter of life and death. With our combined skills, wit, and determination, we needed to be ready to face whatever lay ahead.

Chapter 17

The mysterious chants and the fervour of the ritual continued to rise, reaching a fevered pitch that resonated through the very stone and soil of the rainforest. Nadia and I perched high above the scene and watched with bated breath, the energy of the ritual pulling at us, almost calling us to join in. But something held us back— a feeling of dread, of something not quite right.

Below, the flames leapt and danced, moving in unison with the gathered crowd, all swaying to the rhythm of some ancient beat. And at the centre of it all, the man tied to the rock, his eyes ablaze with a fire that was not of this world.

"The transformation," I whispered, my voice barely audible above the growing cacophony. "It's almost complete. Deimos has altered his DNA."

Nadia's eyes widened as she realized the gravity of what was happening before us. "You mean he's…"

"Yes," I nodded, my voice tight with tension. "He's creating a demigod. But there's more to it. Look at the ritual. Look at the symbols. This isn't just about power. Deimos is… he's building something more."

The spectacle below unfolded with chilling precision. The gathered followers, their faces hidden behind dark masks, moved as one, their chants growing louder, their movements more fervent. It was mesmerizing and terrifying all at once.

"Creating a demigod isn't enough for him," Nadia said, her voice filled with a mix of awe and fear. "He's launching a cult. This is all a part of some grand design."

We continued to watch, unable to tear our eyes away from the unfolding drama below. The man tied to the rock, his body wracked with the pain of transformation, began to move, his limbs stretching, his muscles rippling. The flames responded, swirling around him, bending to his will.

"It's working," I breathed the words in a whisper in the wind. "He's controlling the flames."

"Deimos is succeeding," Nadia replied, her voice filled with a mix of wonder and terror. "But why the rituals? Why the symbolism? An Ancient doesn't need these theatrics."

I pondered her words, my mind racing as I tried to make sense of what we were witnessing. "Maybe that's the point," I finally said. "The theatrics, the rituals, are all part of his plan. He's not just creating a demigod; he's creating a myth. He's capturing human fantasy, building something that will resonate with people, draw them in."

"A cult," Nadia repeated, the word heavy with meaning.

"Yes," I nodded, my mind working through the implications. "But not just any cult. A cult that could change the world that could reshape reality itself."

We watched in silence as the ritual reached its climax. The followers below, their voices raised in a triumphant chorus, moved as one, their bodies and the flames moving in a beautiful and terrifying dance. And at the centre of it all, the man, now something more than human, his body glowing with an otherworldly light, his eyes filled with a power that was not of this earth.

"He's done it," Nadia whispered, her voice filled with awe. "He's extinguished the flames."

"Yes," I replied, my heart pounding in my chest. "But what has he unleashed?"

We sat silently, the weight of what we had witnessed settling over us like a heavy blanket. Deimos had succeeded. He had created a demigod and had launched a cult that could change the very fabric of our world. But to what end?

"Deimos always thinks steps ahead," I said, my voice quiet, my thoughts heavy. "This is just the beginning. There's something more, something bigger. He's planning something that we can't even begin to understand."

Nadia nodded, her face pale, her eyes wide. "We need to stop him. We need to find a way to undo what he's done."

"We will," I said, my voice filled with a determination that I didn't quite feel. "We have to."

We sat in silence, the weight of our mission, the gravity of what we were facing settling over us. The game had become real, the stakes higher than we could have ever imagined. Deimos had unleashed something powerful, something that could change the world.

And it was up to us to stop him.

With heavy hearts and minds filled with questions, we began our descent, the temple and the forest now feeling like a living, breathing entity, watching us, waiting. The path ahead was filled with danger and uncertainty, and we were right in the thick of it. But we knew that we had to move forward to face the unknown.

Our skills, our coordination, and our determination were all that stood between Deimos and his dark ambitions.

But we were ready. We had to be.

For the world, for ourselves, we would face whatever lay ahead. The battle had only just begun.

The darkness of the rainforest was both a cloak and a maze, filled with twisted shadows and hidden dangers. As we made our way through the dense foliage, the events at the temple continued to haunt our minds, echoing like the distant drums of the ritual.

"What do you think Deimos's endgame is?" Nadia asked, her voice barely above a whisper, her eyes scanning the darkness.

"I'm not sure," I admitted, my mind still struggling to comprehend what we had witnessed. "But whatever it is, it's something big, something that could change the very nature of our world."

"We need to find answers," Nadia said, her voice filled with determination. "We need to find out what he's planning and stop him before it's too late."

"Yes," I agreed, my resolve hardening. "But how?"

"We need to get closer," Nadia said, her voice thoughtful. "We need to find a way into his inner circle, understand what he's doing, and unravel his plans from the inside."

I looked at her, my eyes widening at the thought. "That's dangerous," I said, my voice filled with concern.

"It's the only way," Nadia said, her eyes meeting mine, filled with a determination that left no room for doubt. "We need to become a part of his world, to see it from the inside. Only then can we truly understand what he's planning."

I knew she was right, but the thought of infiltrating Deimos's inner circle, of becoming a part of his world, filled me with a fear that was both real and primal. But I also knew that it was the only way. We had to face our fears, take risks, and do whatever it took to stop him.

"We'll do it," I said, my voice filled with a determination that matched hers. "We'll find a way in. We'll stop him."

We continued on, our path lit only by the faint glow of the moon, our minds filled with the gravity of our mission. The rainforest was alive with the sounds of the night, the chirping of insects, the rustling of leaves, and the distant calls of unknown creatures. But there was something else, something hidden, something watching.

We made our way to a hidden cave we had discovered earlier, a place that would serve as our base of operations. As we settled in, the weight of our mission, the enormity of what lay ahead, began to settle over us.

"We need to be careful," I said, my voice filled with the weight of our task. "We need to be smart. Deimos is powerful, and he has eyes everywhere. We can't afford to make a mistake."

"We won't," Nadia said, her voice filled with quiet confidence. "We'll be careful. We'll be smart. We'll find a way in, and we'll stop him."

I looked at her, my eyes meeting hers, filled with a confidence that left no room for doubt. "Yes," I said, my voice stern with conviction. "We will."

We settled into our makeshift camp, the darkness of the cave a comforting blanket, the sounds of the night a soothing lullaby. But sleep was elusive, our minds filled with the weight of our task, the enormity of what lay ahead.

As I lay there, my thoughts drifting, the image of the man at the centre of the ritual, his body wracked with the pain of transformation, his eyes filled with a power that was not of this world, kept haunting me.

What had Deimos unleashed? What was he planning? What did he hope to achieve?

I knew that the answers were out there, hidden in the shadows, waiting to be discovered. But I also knew that finding them would not be easy. The path ahead was filled with danger and uncertainty, the stakes higher than we could have ever imagined.

But we were ready. We had to be. We would face all that stood between Deimos and his dark ambitions. For the world, for ourselves. The battle had only just begun, and we were ready to dance.

* * *

Nadia and I crouched in the dim recesses of the cave, our breaths catching in the thick silence as we prepared for our first-ever astral briefing with Captain Hills and Colonel Mariani. The weight of the unknown lay heavy on our shoulders, yet the absurdity of it all, the odd mix of rituals and Deimos's grand plan to create a demigod lightened the mood. An evil Ancient launching a cult? It sounded like the plot of a bad novel.

"Ready to drop this bombshell on them?" Nadia asked, her eyes twinkling with mischief.

"I hope they're sitting down," I replied, a grin tugging at my lips. "Or floating, or whatever people do in the astral plane."

We shared a brief chuckle, our spirits buoyed by our shared sense of humour, before settling into the intense focus required for the astral meeting. The danger was real, our protective barriers essential, but we wouldn't let it dampen our spirits.

With our minds intertwined, we reached across the astral

plane, connecting with the consciousness of Hills and Mariani. The connection was surreal, a meeting of minds in a space beyond space, but we were prepared.

"Ah, there you are," Hills' voice rang out, warm and teasing. "We were starting to think you'd gotten lost."

"Only in Sophie's endless musings about the fashion choices of evil Ancients," Nadia quipped, her tone playful.

I could almost hear Mariani's mental chuckle. "I knew I was missing out on something important."

"All jokes aside," I said, reigning in the banter, "we've discovered something big. Something… unexpected."

The humour gave way to seriousness as we relayed our findings. Deimos's odd mix of rituals, his pupil's scenic transformation, and the cult's looming threat. It was a lot to take in, and the silence that followed was thick with tension.

"A cult?" Mariani finally asked, disbelief evident in his voice. "You're serious?"

"As serious as Deimos's fashion sense," Nadia replied, unable to resist.

Mariani's laughter broke the tension. "That's very serious indeed."

"We should infiltrate the cult," I suggested, my tone determined. "Get to the heart of it."

"Slow down," Mariani cautioned, his voice firm. "We need more planning, more information. This changes everything."

"You mean we don't get to wear the silly cult robes?" Nadia interjected, her tone feigning disappointment.

"Not yet," Mariani replied, amusement in his echoing voice. "Return to the academy. We'll regroup and hammer down a more detailed plan."

With a final round of good-natured ribbing, we ended the

astral meeting, our connection severed, our minds returning to our bodies in the cave. The weight of what lay ahead was still there, but the levity of our banter lingered, a reminder that even in the face of darkness, we could find light.

As Nadia and I walked back past the protection shield, our powers ready to teleport us back to the academy, we shared a knowing look.

"Ready for whatever comes next?" she asked, her eyes shining with determination.

"Always," I replied, a grin on my face. "As long as it doesn't involve silly hats."

With a flash, we were gone, back to the academy, our path clear, our resolve unbreakable.

Facing an Ancient with plans for chaos and cults was no small feat, but we were ready.

And, most importantly, we hadn't lost our sense of humour.

Bring on the next chapter. We were just getting started.

Chapter 18

With the day's revelations weighing heavily on my mind, I flopped onto my bed, staring at the ceiling as if it might offer some grand insight into the twisted plans of Deimos. A cult, a demigod, an Ancient with an eye for theatrics and a penchant for convoluted rituals? It was like something out of one of my weirdest dreams.

The silence of my room was broken only by the soft rustling of pages as I reviewed the information collected during the last mission. Comparing those details with what Phoebe had told me in our initial encounters, it was clear that things had evolved beyond any expectations.

"Speaking of weird dreams," I muttered to myself, a thought forming. "Maybe it's time to call in my favourite fashion consultant."

As if summoned by my very thoughts, Phoebe materialized beside me, her form as elegant as ever. "Did someone call for a fashion consultant, or was that just a wild guess on my part?"

I grinned, turning to face her. "Phoebe! Just the ancient I wanted to see."

Phoebe's eyes twinkled with amusement. "Ancient? Darling, you wound me. I prefer 'timelessly fabulous.'"

I laughed, the tension in my chest easing at her familiar

banter. "Timelessly fabulous it is. You should consider a career in marketing."

"Oh, I have," she replied, her voice dripping with mock seriousness. "But the pay is dreadfully dull."

We shared a laugh, the warmth of her presence soothing the anxiety of the day. The connection between us was a welcoming comfort, and her humour was the perfect antidote to the weight of the mission.

"You seem troubled, dear," Phoebe said, her tone softening. "What's on your mind?"

I sighed, running a hand through my hair. "Deimos's plan. It's all so… complicated. A cult, a demigod, rituals that make no sense. And why a pupil? Why not just create chaos himself?"

Phoebe floated closer, her hand reaching out as if to comfort me. "Ah, the mind of an Ancient. Always one for theatrics and complexity. It's like a never-ending soap opera."

"A soap opera?" I asked, my curiosity piqued. "Do you think Deimos has a flair for the dramatic?"

Phoebe's laughter rang through the room. "Darling, if Ancient history were a fashion show, Deimos would be the one strutting down the runway in the most outrageous ensemble imaginable."

I chuckled, the imagery too perfect. "So, what you're saying is, we need to out-strut him?"

Phoebe's eyes sparkled. "Exactly. Out-strut, out-dazzle, and outmanoeuvre. But remember, darling, all with impeccable taste."

Phoebe's wisdom, coated with banter, was precisely what I needed. With renewed determination, I returned to my notes, Phoebe's words echoing in my mind.

A cult, a demigod, and an Ancient with a flair for the

dramatic? Bring it on.

We had plans to make a cult to infiltrate and a runway to conquer.

And as Phoebe would say, we would do it all with impeccable taste.

"Ready to out-dazzle Deimos?" I asked, looking up at Phoebe.

Her smile was radiant. "Always, darling. Always."

With that, we dove back into our planning, our laughter filling the room. The more we spoke, the lighter the pressure of the mission became.

Facing an Ancient had never been so fabulous.

We continued to analyze the documents, maps, and information, and the night went on. Phoebe, the Ancient Titanness, proved to be a remarkable partner. Her profound wisdom and quick humour kept the atmosphere lively.

"Look at this ritual," I said, squinting at a diagram. "It's like Deimos threw a bunch of symbols together and hoped something magical would come out."

Phoebe chuckled, leaning closer. "That's the Ancients for you. Always experimenting. Some of their combinations would give even the most avant-garde artists pause."

I snorted, picturing Deimos on the cover of some celestial fashion magazine, his rituals labelled as the "season's hottest trend."

"And this one," I continued, pointing to another arcane drawing. "It looks like dance steps. Think Deimos does a little jig while performing his rituals?"

Phoebe burst out laughing. "I'd pay to see that. An Ancient, all-powerful and fearsome, prancing around like a ballerina."

We dissolved into chuckles, the image too absurd to ignore.

Eventually, our giggles subsided, and Phoebe grew more

serious. "Sophie, we can make fun, but there's logic to this chaos. These rituals, these symbols, they're part of a grand design. Deimos isn't playing; he's constructing something formidable."

Her words struck me, and I knew she was right. The levity had been a pleasant diversion, but the significance of the situation remained.

"You're right," I said, my voice quiet. "We need to solve this puzzle. We need to understand what he's planning and what this cult means. We have to infiltrate."

Phoebe's hand touched mine, her voice tender. "We will, my dear. We'll outsmart him. We'll dazzle him, remember?"

Her conviction lifted me, and I nodded. "We'll out-dazzle him."

We returned to our research with renewed focus, our laughter replaced by concentration and resolve. The night wore on with the soft sounds of papers rustling and our voices whispering.

As dawn neared, I leaned back, exhaustion weighing on me—Phoebe, timeless Ancient that she was, remained beside me, a reassuring presence.

"We'll find a way," I murmured.

"We will," she replied with a gentle smile. "And we'll do it with panache."

With that, I closed my eyes, Phoebe's vow lingering, a glimmer of hope in the darkness.

Deimos had his rituals, his cult, and his grand scheme.

But we had something more potent.

We had each other.

And as Phoebe would affirm, we had exquisite taste.

The battle was only beginning, but we were prepared.

We would triumph with flair.

Chapter 19

"Okay, listen up, you two," Captain Ramona Hills said as she spread a collection of parchment-like papers across the conference table. "I want to hear what you've got. And before you ask, yes, I've made sure we're out of earshot of anyone who shouldn't hear us. We're as secluded as a trio of teenagers plotting to steal cookies from the school kitchen."

I grinned at Nadia, who rolled her eyes but returned the smile. "Cookies? I thought we were saving the world, not indulging in culinary crimes," she quipped.

"Yeah, well, some of us multitask," Hills shot back, tapping the papers with a finger. "Now spill. What have you learned?"

Taking my cue, I leaned forward, excitement bubbling within me. "Deimos isn't just throwing a mystical party with voodoo dolls and pentagrams. No, he's planning something bigger. He's going full Messiah. Only his version of turning water into wine would probably involve turning people into minions."

Nadia picked up the thread. "Exactly. I've been diving into ancient scripts, prophecies, and gossip columns from the last three millennia. The pattern is clear: Deimos wants to reinvent himself as a religious icon. Imagine combining the charisma of a TV evangelist with the pyrotechnics of a rock star. That's

Deimos, only with real fire and brimstone."

Hills raised an eyebrow, amused yet concerned. "So what you're saying is we're not just dealing with a cult, but also a superstar Ancient who's eyeing a career in religion?"

"Precisely," I said, nodding, "think about it. Deimos has the Ancient magic for the 'wow' factor. He's recruiting human disciples to show he's still in touch with the mortal realm. And he's creating rituals that are a cross between a rock concert and a revivalist tent meeting. The guy's not messing around. He's planning to show up as himself, as the big, bad Ancient, to instil fear and recruit followers through that fear. It's like Conspiracy 101, but the professor can actually levitate."

"Sounds like the sort of drama that'd give daytime soaps a run for their money," Hills mused. "Except with apocalyptic implications, of course."

Nadia chuckled. "Imagine the season finale. Spoiler alert: Everyone gets enslaved or turns into a doomsday prepper. The choice is yours."

Hills sighed, clearly grappling with the gravity of our findings. "You realize that this complicates the matter? If he succeeds in setting up this cult, amassing believers through miracles and fear, we won't just be fighting Deimos. We'll be fighting a whole following who believe he's their saviour."

"Yeah, so we need to stop him before he gets to the first hymn," I said, "or before he sends his first tweet, whatever comes first. Imagine his hashtag: #DeimosDelivers or maybe #BowBeforeYourNewGod. I can already see it trending."

Nadia and I shared a laugh before Hills audibly cleared her throat, snapping us back to reality. "Look, I understand this is a coping mechanism for you two, but don't forget the severity of this situation. We're looking at a potential religious uprising supported by an Ancient power. We've got to stop him before he goes public and certainly before he starts his own YouTube channel."

We both nodded, the humour fading from our faces. Hills was right. Our jesting might keep our spirits up, but it wouldn't save the world.

"So, what's the plan?" Nadia asked. "We can't just crash his cult party shouting, 'Surprise, the gig's up!'"

Hills folded her arms, contemplating. "We need to strategise. Gather more intel. Figure out how to counter his narrative before it gains traction. And I hate to say it, but we may have to consider revealing our powers to the world to show another side to this ancient coin."

"We'll have to do it with finesse," I added. "You know, just casually float in the air during a live news broadcast or teleport into a world leaders' summit. 'Hey guys, put those nukes away. We have magic.'"

Hills smirked. "You may be onto something there. But it's a one-shot deal. It has to be perfect."

"We'll make sure of it," Nadia affirmed.

The three of us locked eyes, knowing we were committed to this strange, terrifying, and oddly exhilarating mission.

"So," Hills began, breaking the heavy moment, "who's going to draft the mission statement, and who's getting the cookies?"

The tension in the room broke as we erupted in laughter. Cookies or not, we had a world to save. And by gods and Ancients, we'd save it with style.

* * *

As our astral forms settled into this dreamscape's misty, kaleidoscopic realm—name and owner yet to be identified—I was awestruck. It was like floating in a space that was a fusion of a surrealist painting and a Pink Floyd music video. Walls melted and reformed into different shapes, and clouds that tasted like cotton candy floated by. Yes, tasted; senses were more like suggestions in the astral plane.

"Wow, this guy's subconscious is a straight-up art gallery. Look at those colours!" Nadia seemed equally impressed, her eyes widening as if trying to absorb the vibrant palette around us.

"And look at the ground! Is that…vinyl records? With classical etchings?" I poked the ground, which emitted a soft melody as if each record was its own interactive playlist.

Before we could dive deeper into the art installation that was this dreamscape, the dreamer himself appeared. Materializing in a burst of light, he wore a T-shirt that read, 'Existential Crisis Loading… Please Wait.'

"Hey! Who are you two?" he asked. "Are you figments of my imagination? Freudian projections? Darn, did I eat too much cheese again before bed?"

Nadia chuckled. "Freudian projections? If that were the case, we'd probably be here discussing your relationship with your mother or something equally awkward. Nah, more like spiritual auditors. We're here to check your existential balance sheet."

"Okay, let's put names to these so-called 'auditors.' I'm Sophie, and this is Nadia," I jumped in, grinning. "We're as real as your doubts about reality. If we were food, I'd be the spicy tuna roll—full of surprises and a hint of kick."

"And I'd be the dependable but zesty chicken wing. Good in any situation," Nadia added.

He laughed, his dream-state eyes twinkling. "Alright, I can dig the food metaphors. So, I'm Josh. Josh Duarte. Just a 19-year-old from LA trying to navigate this whole 'life' thing. So, Spicy Tuna Roll and Zesty Chicken Wing, what brings you into my dreams?"

"Nailed it, Josh. Okay, you asked, so here goes," I said, diving right into it. "We've come to chat about your new apprenticeship with Deimos. I've got to say, mastering fire tricks and ancient rituals is a rather peculiar career choice."

He tilted his head, looking both puzzled and intrigued. "Career choice? Look, Deimos has shown me a path to make the world better. So, you're like, astral career advisors or something?"

Nadia grinned. "Astral career advisors? That's a new one. We're offering something more substantial—a reality check, to be precise."

As we bantered, Josh started to grow more comfortable, and why wouldn't he? We were in his subconscious gallery of dreams, after all. "Okay, fine. I'm intrigued but not sold. What's your pitch?"

"Simple," I replied, the dreamscape around us starting to coalesce into a cosy fireside chat setup. "We're offering you the chance to question what you've been taught, to weigh your actions and their consequences. Because let me tell you, the path you're walking on right now has more landmines than a military training ground."

"Poetic," Josh said. "And the old adage says, 'With great power comes great responsibility.' Except this isn't a comic book, and you're not my Uncle Ben."

"Right on the money," Nadia added. "Except, unlike comic books, there's no reset button in real life. You get one shot to make it right."

Our astral forms began to vibrate, signalling that our dream rendezvous was coming to an end. "Think about what we've said, Josh. No rush, but also, you know, some urgency wouldn't hurt," I said, locking eyes with him for emphasis.

"Got it," he replied, looking genuinely contemplative. "And if I have more questions, or let's say if I'm considering Team Reality Check?"

"We're just an astral call away," I assured him, smiling. "This might be the dream realm, but our offer is as real as it gets."

With that, our astral selves dissolved, leaving the vibrant landscape of Josh's dreamscape. I felt hopeful as we rematerialized in our focus room back at the academy. Maybe, just maybe, we'd sown the seeds of doubt in a potentially hazardous soil. And sometimes, that's the first step to growing something great.

"So," Nadia broke the silence. "How did we do? Did we just astral-shark tank our way into a win?"

"Too soon to say," I replied. "But hey, at least we didn't get kicked out by dream security. I'd call *that* a win."

And as we both chuckled, settling back into our physical forms, I knew one thing for sure: Whether we'd successfully persuaded Josh or not, we'd made an impact, a ripple in the vast pond of possibilities. And sometimes, that's all you need—a ripple that could lead to a wave of change.

Chapter 20

Josh

I opened my eyes, the lingering impression of an abstract dreamscape still clinging to my mind. That was one hell of a dream. I mean, spicy tuna rolls and zesty chicken wings? My imagination outdid itself this time.

Only wait a sec. This wasn't just my imagination working overtime; these were actual astral projections. Deimos had told me about this stuff, but experiencing it was a whole other story.

My first impulse was to rush to Deimos, spill the beans, and give him the full low-down. Then I stopped, grinning. Why should I ruin the surprise? Deimos had warned me about the academy fools who'd try to mess up his divine plans. A couple of teenagers were his arch-nemesis? That's like telling me my grandma's knitting circle was a front for a secret society. Hilarious.

These girls had no idea what they were up against. Sure, Deimos might look like a cross between a Greek god and an emo rock star, but the guy had serious horsepower under the hood—literal immortal powers. And I was his chosen apprentice, the designated "Messiah." I don't know what will if that doesn't make me the coolest guy in the room.

I sit up in my bed and stretch my arms above my head, glancing at the view outside my window before comfortably dropping them on the covers, still chuckling.

Spicy Tuna Roll and Zesty Chicken Wing had no clue what they'd gotten themselves into. This was going to be a hoot. It was like playing chess with someone who didn't even know how the horsey moved. Oops, I mean knight. See? I know chess terminology. I'm a cultured future demigod here.

Now, how should I play this out? Straight-up blasting them off the astral plane would be too easy. Like taking candy from a baby, or in my case, making it disappear and then laughing as the baby throws a fit. No, I had to savour this—toy with them, like a cat batting at a half-dead mouse. There's an art to being diabolically evil, and I wanted to be the Picasso of malevolence.

Aha, I've got it! I'll be Mr. Charming, the friendly and naive apprentice just "searching for his path," as they put it. I'll make them think they're actually getting through to me. Let them dream of turning me away from Deimos. Then, when they least expect it—BOOM! Unleash hell, in the most literal sense. Oh man, this was going to be so good. I might as well start rehearsing my Academy Award acceptance speech for Best Villain.

I chuckled at the thought. Deimos had talked about causing chaos, generating fear, and imposing the will of Ancient Gods on humanity, and here I was, planning the best pranks for my clueless adversaries. But hey, who said chaos couldn't be fun? I've always believed that a job's not worth doing if you can't have a laugh or two while you're at it. And make no mistake, causing fear and mayhem was definitely my job now.

But just for a second, let's play devil's advocate—or would it be god's advocate in this case? Let's assume these girls weren't totally misguided in their quest to steer me clear of my divine destiny. What could they offer? A life of boring academics and, what, being a good Samaritan? C'mon, where's the glamour in that? I've seen what Deimos can do, the fire he controls, the rituals that defy the laws of physics. Next to that, their "reality check" felt like paying taxes: a dreary but necessary evil of life.

Nah, I've made up my mind.

Deimos is the way to go, and nothing will change that. But for now, I'll let Sophie and Nadia think they're close to winning me over. Let them have their moment under the astral sun before I darken their skies for good.

I glanced over at the digital clock on my nightstand flashing 6:00 AM. Ugh, even potential demigods need their beauty sleep. But first, I had to prepare. Sophie and Nadia would be stepping into a trap they'd never even see coming.

I lay back down, chuckling softly.

They say you should keep your friends close and your enemies closer. Well, Sophie and Nadia were about to find out just how close an enemy could get. And they say I'm the one who needed a reality check? Oh, the delicious irony!

So, with thoughts of my brilliant, albeit nefarious, plan dancing in my head, I settled into my bed. The girls could have their astral plane; I was off to the dreamland, where I was already the hero of my own epic saga. And the best part? The story was just about to get good, so good.

Chapter 21

"You did WHAT, now?" Captain Ramona Hills' eyes flared, narrowing into slits that could pierce through steel as she glared at Sophie and Nadia. Her voice seemed to levitate ominously around the room like an unwelcoming ghost. The captain's gaze made Sophie and Nadia squirm like two kids caught with their hands in the cookie jar—except this jar contained a potential demigod-in-the-making.

Sophie cleared her throat, "Ahem, well, you see… Captain, we took a, um, proactive approach—"

"Proactive approach?" a rough chuckle spilt from Hills' lips. "That's like calling a bull in a china shop an 'interior redecorator.' You were supposed to make a PLAN, not go on a mystical joyride in someone's dreams!"

Nadia chimed in, her eyes glimmering with a defiance that only ancient teens can muster. "We were conducting ground-level intelligence gathering. That's a form of planning, isn't it?"

Hills sighed, pinching the bridge of her nose as if warding off an impending migraine. "You two give a new meaning to the term 'freelancing.' Look, there are protocols for a reason. You can't just gallivant into the astral plane and play therapist to a potentially evil demigod candidate."

Sophie and Nadia exchanged glances, a hint of remorse shadowing their eyes. But before either could speak, Hills continued, her voice softened now, wading into the pools of reason.

"However," she paused for dramatic effect, "some good could come from this reckless endeavour of yours. We just need to steer this ship back on course."

Both girls perked up at that like of two dogs, hearing the rustle of a snack bag.

"You think he's going to 'play nice' to ensnare you, right?" Hills leaned back, folding her arms across her chest. "Well, guess what, my budding double-O agents? I bet our dear Josh here is as much of an idiot as you two are."

Sophie feigned insult, "Hey, I'll have you know, idiocy is a highly underrated survival skill!"

Nadia added, "Seriously, being underestimated is practically a superpower. You should try it sometime."

Hills chuckled, "Oh, don't worry, I've had my fair share of underestimation. But right now, we need to focus. If this Josh thinks he's going to outwit you, why don't we flip the script?"

Sophie's eyes lit up, "You mean, let him think he's entrapping us while we're actually entrapping him?"

"Exactly," Hills smirked. "We play along with his charade. Make him think he's luring you into his lair or whatever he imagines in his self-styled villainous brain. And then, when he least expects it, we spring our actual plan."

Nadia raised an eyebrow, "And what would that plan be? I doubt 'gotcha' would suffice."

Hills steepled her fingers, contemplating. "Our real objective remains the same: find out what Deimos is planning and how far he's willing to go. We need to know if this Josh kid is integral to Deimos' plot. And what better way to find out than letting him think he's won?"

Sophie clapped her hands gleefully, "Ah, the good ol' Trojan Horse tactic, but without the horse. Or Troy. Or—well, you get what I mean."

Nadia grinned, "A honey trap for the mind. I like it."

Hills nodded approvingly, "Very well, let's fine-tune this 'honey trap.' We'll need code words, fallback plans, safe words—"

"Safe words?" Sophie giggled. "This isn't Fifty Shades of Astral Plane, Captain."

Hills rolled her eyes, "For communication, you dimwit. If things go south, you'll need a way to alert us without tipping off Josh."

Nadia suggested, "How about 'spicy tuna roll'? It's so absurd. It's got to work."

Sophie clapped, "Perfect! And it pays homage to our first astral encounter."

The trio dove into planning, detailing each step of their intricate operation. The room is filled with scribbles, doodles, and the occasional snack break because even secret agents need fuel. They laughed, they debated, and most importantly, they prepared. If Josh thought he would outwit them, he had another thing coming.

After what seemed like an eternity, Hills finally looked up from the heap of notes scattered across the table. "I think we've got ourselves a plan. If this doesn't work, well, at least we'll go down as the most entertaining disaster in the annals of the academy."

Sophie and Nadia chuckled. Despite the gravity of the

situation, the levity felt good, like a breath of fresh air in a smoke-filled room.

"Alright, double-O dingbats," Hills stood up, gathering the piles of paper. "Get some rest. You've got a big night ahead in Dreamland."

As they exited the meeting room, the weight of their task slightly lightened by their camaraderie, Sophie turned to Nadia, "Do you think we can pull this off?"

Nadia grinned, her eyes twinkling with that ancient teen mischief, "Oh, we're going to give Mr. Duarte a show he'll never forget."

And just like that, they walked off, leaving the room filled with the echoes of their laughter, their plan laid out like a map to buried treasure. Little did they know, they were the treasure—two gems of wit and courage in a world desperately in need of light. Whether they realized it or not, they were about to embark on an adventure that could very well decide the fate of not just one but multiple worlds.

Captain Ramona Hills stood alone in the now-empty room, a proud smile crossing her face. "Godspeed, you crazy kids," she muttered almost reverently. "Godspeed."

So there it was—the making of a most unlikely fellowship, armed with code words and an audacious plan, ready to take on a self-proclaimed demigod and his delusional mentor. Their hopes rested on their ability to outwit the outwitter, to entrap the entraper. It was a game of cosmic chess, and they were ready to play. Even if they weren't entirely sure how the "horsey moved."

And if they failed? Well, they would certainly give new meaning to the phrase "It's so crazy, it just might work." Or not. But hey, that's a story for another chapter.

* * *

Sophie and Nadia stood in the training grounds, eyes narrowed and guns drawn. Their sniper rifles glinted in the sunlight as they peered through the scopes, each aiming for a far-off target. With almost supernatural precision, they squeezed the triggers. Two almost simultaneous shots rang out, and two targets burst into a cloud of faux smoke and glitter. You see, in their training world, even a miss could be fabulous.

"Nice shot, kiddo," Sophie grinned, lowering her rifle.

"Likewise, grandma," Nadia retorted. She might have the spirit of an ancient goddess, but the snark was all teen.

Next on the docket: hand-to-hand combat. They discarded their sniper rifles and got into their respective fighting stances. Sophie lunged first, throwing a punch that seemed like it was pulled from the matrix. Nadia ducked and countered with a high kick that whizzed past Sophie's head, messing up her perfectly coiffed hair.

"Hey, watch the hair! You know how long it takes to look this effortlessly dishevelled?" Sophie complained, attempting to swat Nadia away like an annoying fly.

Nadia giggled, "As long as it took you to find that sentence in a hipster magazine?"

Before Sophie could retort, she found herself dodging an incoming energy bolt from Nadia's outstretched palm. The bolt zapped past her, scorching a nearby target into a pile of ashes.

"Elemental fighting time already?" Sophie smirked, wiping imaginary sweat from her forehead.

Nadia shrugged, "I felt inspired."

Both floated off the ground, hovering a few feet in the air.

Sophie conjured fireballs in her hands, spinning them like a circus performer before hurling them towards Nadia. Nadia deflected them with gusts of wind, creating a mini-tornado that sucked up the fireballs and extinguished them.

"Ah, air versus fire. Classic elemental banter!" Sophie chortled.

"Wait for it," Nadia grinned, her eyes glinting with mischief.

Suddenly, she unleashed torrents of water, shaping them into aquatic missiles aimed straight at Sophie. But Sophie was quick. She retaliated by turning the fire in her palms to shards of ice, meeting Nadia's water midway. Steam erupted from the collision, enveloping them both in a misty haze.

Just as they were about to resume—Nadia gearing up to form mini-thunderclouds and Sophie creating an earthen shield—both felt an intrusive mental ping so loud, it almost drowned out their thoughts.

"Hey, foodies, we need to talk!"

The voice echoed through their minds like an obnoxious radio jingle you can't get out of your head. Both girls lost focus, spiralling briefly before crashing down to the ground like two sacks of magical potatoes.

Sophie groaned, "Did someone just text our brains?"

Nadia dusted herself off, "If they did, they need to work on their message tone. I felt like my head was inside a subwoofer."

The psychic intrusion was, of course, courtesy of Josh, who seemed to lack the fine art of subtlety. It was like receiving a mental 'U Up?' message, but from someone you'd rather not dream about, let alone meet in a dream.

Sophie rolled her eyes, "Ah, the culinary stylings of Mr. Duarte. I suppose our astral tête-à-tête has earned us a VIP pass to his mind."

Nadia frowned, "He sure knows how to crash a party, doesn't he?"

For a moment, both girls stood in silence, pondering their next move. The astral summoning couldn't be ignored, especially given their newly minted plan of engaging with Josh and his manic mentor.

Finally, Sophie broke the silence, "Alright, let's hear what Chef Duarte has to cook up."

Nadia nodded, "But first, I'm putting up mental do-not-disturb signs. If he thinks he can just barge into our minds like a bad pop-up ad, he's got another thing coming."

Both took deep breaths, steadying their hearts and minds. With a shared glance that spoke a thousand words, they prepared to re-enter the treacherous landscape of Josh Duarte's psyche. Their training session might have been rudely interrupted, but in their world, every moment was a step closer to understanding and defeating the obscure plots that lay ahead.

As they braced themselves for whatever awaited them in the astral plane, Sophie couldn't help but think that their lives were increasingly resembling a comic book. And in that comic book, she and Nadia were the superheroes—complete with elemental powers and snappy one-liners.

Only time would tell if their 'dynamic duo' act could bring down a would-be demigod and save not just one but perhaps many worlds from a catastrophe too terrible to imagine. So, like the heroes they were shaping up to be, they plunged forward, bolstered by their newfound camaraderie, ready to face the uncertain future.

In the real world, they looked like two students who'd just hit the library for some serious cramming. But they were warriors in the making in the multiple dimensions and planes that lay beyond. And as every warrior knows, the journey of a thousand battles begins with a single, strategically fired shot—or, in their case, an intrusive astral text message from an increasingly annoying antagonist.

"Bring it on, Josh," Sophie muttered under her breath as they closed their eyes and let their minds drift away, ready for the next chapter of their evolving saga. "Bring it on."

* * *

Our story will unfold in its first clash in the next book: "The game is on".

About the Author

Joe McFrancis is a husband and a father living in rural Ireland. He is an experienced technical author specialising in corporate software architecture design and, on the side, games development. However, he always wanted to write for fun, so he finally did it. Joe loves Fantasy and SciFi stories. He had this idea about Sophie, so he brought her adventure to life with his family's help and collaboration.

You can connect with me on:
🌐 https://joemcfrancis.com

Subscribe to my newsletter:
✉ https://joemcfrancis.com/newsletter